DEADLY DARE

What am I going to do?

I've got to do *something*. If I don't, Tom will end up in trouble – in prison, or worse. I've got to look out for my brother. He may be a lot older than me but he sure isn't smarter. Anyone with half an eye could see that he and the rest of the gang are up to something. Knowing Scott, Robbie's brother, it's something illegal. Knowing Robbie, it wouldn't surprise me if someone ended up dead. I just don't want it to be Tom – or me.

Hippo Mystery

DEADLY DARE

Malorie Blackman

Hippo

Scholastic Children's Books
7–9 Pratt Street, London NW1 0AE, UK
a division of Scholastic Publications Ltd
London ~ New York ~ Toronto ~ Sydney ~ Auckland

First published by Scholastic Publications Ltd, 1995

Text copyright © Oneta Malorie Blackman, 1995

ISBN 0 590 13162 1

For Neil, with love

CONTENTS

1 DEAR DIARY

23:35 hrs Wednesday, 14th May

I don't know what to do. Tom just won't listen to me. He says we need the money and this is the only way to get it. I told him I didn't like his friends – especially that Robbie. He's the kind who'd cosh you over the head for a packet of crisps. In fact, he'd cosh you over the head for free, just 'cause he'd have fun doing it. But Tom just laughs at me when I say that.

What am I going to do?

It's past midnight and Tom's still down there with them – his so-called friends. He looks up every ten minutes or so and smiles at me. He doesn't notice that I don't smile back.

I wish I could get through to him. I wish I could keep him away from them.

What am I going to do?

I've got to do *something*. If I don't, Tom will end up in trouble – in prison, or worse. I've got to look out for my brother. He may be a lot older than me but he sure isn't smarter. Anyone with half an eye could see that he and the rest of the gang are up to something. Knowing Scott, Robbie's brother, it's something illegal. Scott doesn't say much but you can see his mind never stops working.

I don't like him either. He gives me the creeps.

He's always smiling, smiling, smiling. I don't trust people who smile all the time when there's nothing to smile about. In a strange way, I think he's worse than Robbie. I know Tom and the rest are up to something bad, something dangerous. Someone's going to get hurt. Knowing Robbie, it wouldn't surprise me if someone ended up dead. I just don't want it to be Tom – or me.

2 THE GAME BEGINS

This was it! Today was the day! Theo was about to make some *serious* money. His brown-black eyes gleamed at the thought. Today was definitely *his* day! And if his head would just stop pounding and his body would stop aching, then there'd be no doubt about it at all!

"Ai ... ai ... aischoo!" Theo's sneeze rang out through the classroom. Followed by another, then another.

Mrs Daltry glared at him. "How much longer d'you intend to inflict your flu germs on us, Theo?" she snapped.

"Sorry, Mrs Daltry." Theo took an already

soggy tissue out of his trouser pocket and wiped his nose.

"Sorry isn't good enough. You should've stayed at home."

Ricky, Theo's best friend, kicked him under the table.

"Ow!" Theo yelled.

"What's the matter now?" frowned the teacher.

"Er … I got a sudden pain in my … er … leg," Theo mumbled.

He glared at Ricky, who was bent over his workbook, writing furiously.

"Theo, if your flu isn't any better tomorrow, stay at home! And if I catch your germs, I won't be best pleased," said Mrs Daltry.

Moany old trout! Theo scowled at her as she turned away. But what did he expect? Sympathy?

"Bless you!" Ricky whispered. It was better late than never!

Theo nodded and sniffed heavily. There was no doubt about it. His rotten cold was getting worse. But there was no way he was going to let a cold stand between him and how much? Twenty odd pounds? Maybe even thirty? And what an easy way to get it! All he had to do was perform a couple of dares and the money was his. It was already as good as in his pocket. What would he do with the money? Theo closed his eyes and smiled as he considered all the possibilities. He could put it towards the cost of a video game, or start saving up for a new bike, or maybe he could buy that ice-cool jacket he'd seen down the precinct.

Theo glanced over at the clock on the wall. Mrs Daltry's Maths lesson was dragging on even more than usual today – something Theo wouldn't have thought was possible.

"Angela, that's the third time you've yawned in five minutes," Mrs Daltry frowned.

"Sorry, Mrs Daltry," Angela said quickly.

"Keeping you awake, am I?" the teacher asked with sarcasm.

Barely! Theo answered Mrs Daltry's question in his head. He could well understand why Angela was yawning!

"What each of you learns here in this classroom will serve you for the rest of your lives. You children have to realize that life is not a bowl of cherries."

A few indistinct murmurs floated in the air. Mrs Daltry had inflicted her favourite saying on the class yet again. Not a day passed without her commenting on life and bowls of cherries at least three times!

"Come on. Come on," Theo muttered, his eyes returning to the clock. Why didn't the buzzer hurry up and sound?

"Theo, did you say something?" Mrs Daltry enquired.

"No, Mrs Daltry," Theo replied quickly.

Today was not the day to wind up the teacher. Already, Theo could feel the others in the class glaring at him. He quickly looked down at his workbook, his face burning. He hated being looked at.

"Hhmm!" Mrs Daltry pursed her lips. Just as she opened her mouth to add more to her suspicious "Hhmm!", the lunch-time buzzer sounded.

"Exercise 24 is homework. I want it in first

thing on Monday morning from *everyone* and no excuses. And for those of you who haven't already done so, don't forget to bring in your consent forms signed by a parent or guardian for next Friday's trip to the Irving Museum to see the Astral Collection. That's the Greek and Roman jewellery exhibition that's on there at the moment. It's very interesting. Very interesting indeed. Some of the pieces are priceless."

The muttering that filled the classroom showed that not many people agreed with the teacher's assessment of the jewellery exhibition. Words like "dull", "tedious" and "yawn" floated down to the front of the class.

"There's also a computer exhibition, hands-on experiments and a space technology exhibition," Mrs Daltry added drily.

The class gave a collective sigh of relief.

"That's more like it," Ricky whispered to Theo.

Theo nodded, watching with everyone else as Mrs Daltry rushed out of the class-room, her packet of liquorice allsorts already out of her jacket pocket.

Cathy ran to the door and popped her head out, looking up and down the corridor.

"All clear," she said at last, giving the rest of the class the thumbs-up. She closed the door and leaned against it.

Ricky whipped his black baseball cap with "CHILL!" written on it out of his bag and put it on. Mrs Daltry didn't let him wear it in class – at least, not when she was teaching.

"OK everyone. It's time to play Cash or Dare! Anyone who's not playing has to leave the class now." Angela Tukesbury made her way to the front of the class.

"Can't we stay and watch?" asked Carl.

"No way. It's against the rules," Angela replied firmly.

Reluctantly, four or five others in the class got to their feet and moved to the door. Ishmar, the last of the non-players, left the classroom, slamming the door petulantly behind him. Cathy leaned against the door again.

"No one's allowed to ask for help from anyone who's just left," ordered Angela.

As Theo watched the new girl he couldn't help frowning. She'd only arrived at the beginning of the week and already it was as if she'd been there for years. There was something about her that Theo wasn't quite sure about. Something about her that he didn't quite like. She had dark brown, almost black, hair and the palest blue eyes Theo had ever seen. Eyes that always seemed to be silently watching you – watching and waiting.

"Theo, are you staying?" Colin asked, surprised.

Theo frowned. He looked at Colin, then around the room. Colin wasn't the only one who was surprised to see him still there.

"Yes, he is staying. What's it to you?" Ricky answered before Theo had the chance.

Theo sighed inwardly. Ricky was his best friend but he did sometimes wish that Ricky didn't insist on fighting all of his battles for him. Theo looked at Ricky, who was still glaring at Colin. Theo and Ricky looked so different. Theo wore round glasses which made him look like a wise owl and was small for his age. He was also too quiet – according to Ricky, Mrs Daltry *and* his parents! No one could say the same thing about Ricky. Ricky was massive, solidly built and almost as tall as Mrs Daltry. He had a loud voice and a louder laugh and no one messed with Ricky. Theo really envied that about him. Nothing and no one scared Ricky. Theo still hadn't given up hoping that maybe just a little of it would rub off on him.

Theo could feel another sneezing fit coming on. He dug into his pocket for his tissue again. It fell apart, damp and clammy around his fingers.

"Ricky, have you got a tissue?" Theo asked, sniffing heavily.

"I've only got the one we used for Legs' hammock this morning," Ricky answered.

Theo wrinkled up his nose. He didn't fancy using the tissue that Ricky's pet tarantula had been swinging in, but beggars couldn't be choosers.

"OK. That'll do," Theo said.

Ricky handed it over.

All at once, a funny-peculiar feeling tickled the back of Theo's neck. He frowned. He knew at once what it was. He was being watched! Theo's head shot up. He was right. Angela was looking straight at him. He knew it! He just knew it! His frown deepened. Angela's eyes burned into his before she looked away, waiting to get everyone's attention. Theo shook his head slowly. There was definitely something about Angela Tukesbury... Still, Cash or Dare was her idea – and Theo had to admit, it was a good one.

"There's twenty-five of us," Ricky said, excitedly. "That means twenty-five pounds."

"And all that money is going into *my* pocket," said Theo, wiping his nose.

"Dream on!" Ricky scoffed.

"This is a great game. We used to play it in my old school," said Angela. "Let's get the money bit over first."

Each member of the class queued up to drop their one pound coins into Angela's plastic cup. Theo and Ricky deliberately stood at the back of the queue. When it was Theo's turn, he peered into the cup before dropping in his money from a greater height than necessary. It made a satisfying *plink* as it hit the other coins. Slowly, he filed back to his desk. Angela smiled and put the cup down beside her.

"The winner of the game will get all this money," she said.

Theo stared at the money cup. Pound coins danced before his eyes. Gold-coloured coins, heavy and glistening.

"The first rule of this game is no one is allowed to let anyone outside of this class-room know what we're doing. Do that and you'll be disqualified immediately." Angela's voice was cool, almost cold.

"These are the other rules of the game," she continued. "We each write down a dare on a piece of paper, fold it twice then drop it in this bag." She held up a Sainsbury's carrier bag. "You mustn't sign your name to it – it's got to be anonymous. Then I'll shake the bag and we each pick out a dare. If you won't or don't do exactly what's written on the paper, then you're out of the game and you lose your pound. No excuses, no reasons, no explanations. If you tell anyone, anyone at all, what your dare is, you're automatically out of the game. Those left after the first round then write out new dares and we go through the whole thing again until only one person is left. And that person gets all this money."

"That's going to be me!" Ricky muttered.

"Hang on a minute. If we're not allowed to tell anyone what our dare is, how is anyone to know whether or not we've done it?" Sarah asked from behind Theo.

"Yeah…"

"That's right…"

All eyes turned towards Angela expectantly.

"If the dare involves someone else, then that person will be a witness. If it's a dare you have to do by yourself, you have to be able to prove that you've done it. Otherwise I'll act as a witness," Angela explained.

"Why you?" Darren asked.

" 'Cause this was my idea and it's my game," Angela replied. "And one more thing – two kinds of dares aren't allowed," she continued.

"Spiteful ones and dangerous ones…"

"What d'you mean by spiteful?"

"And what d'you mean by dangerous?"

Theo was wondering that himself.

"Spiteful is like daring someone to thump someone else. And dangerous is something stupid like daring someone to run out in front of a car or a train. No dorky dares like that are allowed. They've got to have a little imagination behind them. If anyone writes down a dorky dare, the person who picks out that dare doesn't have to do it and automatically goes through to the next round," Angela explained.

"Who's to say whether a dare is dorky or not?" Theo asked.

"I am," Angela replied instantly.

Angela and Theo looked at each other. Theo wanted to ask who'd died and put Angela in charge, but he didn't. If someone else had said it first, then he would've backed them up. Only no one else spoke up either. It looked like everyone was waiting for someone else to do it.

"Remember – no one's allowed to tell any-one outside this class what we're doing. It's our secret," said Angela.

Sarah leaned forward over her desk and tapped Theo on his back.

"Bossy, isn't she?" Sarah whispered.

"That's one word for her," Theo agreed sourly.

"If it was me, I'd let you decide with me whether a dare is dorky or not," Sarah added.

Theo and Ricky exchanged a look. Theo grimaced, kicking Ricky under the table as Ricky put two fingers in his mouth and mimed being violently sick. Theo wondered why Sarah always had to show him up like that? He'd known her since infant school and she was constantly drooling over him. It was *so* embarrassing.

"OK everyone." Angela smiled silkily. "Write down your dares."

Just at that moment, with that secret, silky smile, Angela reminded Theo of Legs, Ricky's tarantula spider, just before it pounced on some unsuspecting insect and gobbled it up.

"What're you going to put?" Ricky asked.

Theo shrugged. "I don't know yet."

"Mine's going to be really *bad*," Ricky gloated. "No one's getting all that money thanks to me!"

"You'd better be careful. You might get your own dare!" Theo pointed out.

Ricky's face fell. "I hadn't thought of that," he said.

"Yeah, well," Theo replied. "You can think of it now!"

Ricky's face dropped even further. Theo chewed his pencil whilst he thought. He hadn't thought of much else since Angela had told everyone about Cash or Dare two days ago. He needed something really good. Something that wasn't dangerous but something that was really difficult. Then it hit him.

"Got one!" Theo announced.

"So have I. A good one," Ricky replied.

Ricky and Theo smirked wickedly at each other. They each bent low over their sheets of paper, their hands cupped secretively around what they were writing. The scratching noises of many pens and pencils moving rapidly across paper filled the room. Cathy, still guarding the door, leaned against it to write down her dare. Theo got a tickle in his throat and coughed impatiently, then coughed again to get rid of it. He'd be glad when his rotten cold went off to torment someone else!

One girl in the class looked around slowly. Everyone was too busy writing to notice her watching. She slipped an already folded piece of paper out of her skirt pocket. Frowning deeply, she looked down at it. Indecision clouded her face.

Come on. Don't chicken out now, she thought sternly.

That was why she'd written down her dare in advance. She knew that if she had to write it down in the class, she'd never go through with it. Her dare was dangerous. Very dangerous. Someone could end up getting hurt, but what other choice did she have?

Do it. Just do it, she told herself.

Her face cleared. Her indecision passed.

Lips pursed with stubborn resolve, she held her pre-prepared dare in her hand, ready to drop it into the carrier bag.

You don't have any choice. She kept repeating that thought in her head, over and over. *You don't have any choice.*

But the frown never left her face.

3 THEO IN TROUBLE

"I feel sorry for the person who gets my dare," Ricky announced to no one in particular.

All the dares had been dropped in the carrier bag. Everyone was jostling for position – no one wanted to be the first or the last to pick one out.

"Right then. I'll give them out now," Angela declared.

"Can't we pick them ourselves?" Sarah protested from beside Theo.

"No, or we'll be here all day," Angela replied. "But first…"

Angela picked up the cup filled with pound

coins and tipped all the money into a small brown envelope before sealing it. She put the envelope in the money belt around her waist. Then she walked about, fishing into the carrier bag and passing out the pieces of paper to the crowd around her. When she gave Theo his dare, she looked at him without smiling, without blinking. Theo frowned. He wished he knew what her problem was. Angela moved on, without saying a word.

Theo stepped back from the crowd and surreptitiously began to unfold his dare. He coughed wearily, wishing his head would stop pounding – just for five seconds.

"Remember, you're not allowed to tell *anyone* what your dare is or you're immediately disqualified," Angela reminded everyone. She took the last dare out of the carrier bag for herself.

No sound could be heard except that of pieces of paper being rustled as they were unfolded. In the next moment, the protests erupted virtually simultaneously. Theo's mouth fell open. He gasped. Groans and cries like "What ratbag wrote down this one?!" filled the room. Theo looked at Ricky. Ricky's face was all scrunched up as if he was chewing a lemon, peel and all.

"Your dare can't be any worse than mine," Theo informed him.

"Wanna bet?" Ricky scowled.

No, Theo didn't want to bet. It would be too easy to win. He grimaced as he looked down at his dare again.

At exactly ten minutes to midnight tonight, you must enter the deserted warehouse at 117 Buzan Road, behind the shopping precinct. You must enter the ventilation shaft at the side of the building and crawl inside QUIETLY. Crawl to the end of the tunnel — no turning off into the tunnels which branch to the right or left. Keep straight. Once you've reached the end of the tunnel, you must wait for an hour until 1 a.m. then leave QUIETLY. If you don't stay for the full hour, you lose. I'll be watching…

Who'll be watching? Frowning, Theo looked around the room. Who could've written this one? Theo caught Sarah's eye and she smiled at him. Theo quickly looked away. Was it her? But hang on, how could Sarah know that he would get her dare? That didn't make any sense at all.

Midnight! Somehow he had to get past his mum and dad and get out of the house to be at – where was it again? – 117 Buzan Road at midnight. It might've seemed like more of an adventure and less like mission impossible if his head and nose hadn't felt like they were stuffed full of cotton wool. The aches in his arms and legs were spreading to his fingers and toes. Everything was hurting! Even his fingernails.

"What's going on in here?"

Theo was so caught up in his dare that he hadn't even heard the classroom door open. Cathy had abandoned her post the moment Angela had handed her a dare and here was the result. Mrs Daltry stood in the doorway, her eyes narrow slits of suspicion.

No one spoke.

"Angela, tell me what's going on in here," Mrs Daltry commanded.

"Nothing, Mrs Daltry. I was just telling everyone about my old school," Angela replied.

She looked so convincingly innocent that she almost had Theo believing she was telling the truth, and he knew better!

"It must have been riveting for everyone to give up their lunch to hear it," Mrs Daltry said.

"I was just telling everyone about a boy in my old class who insisted he'd been kidnapped by aliens. He said he'd been away for over a year but that the aliens went back in time to return him to his bed only an hour after they'd taken him. But the funny thing was…"

"That's quite enough of that nonsense, Angela," Mrs Daltry frowned. "Everyone – out! All of you! I shouldn't have to tell you to go to lunch."

The teacher waited by the door as everyone

trooped past her. Ricky and Theo were practically the last to leave. Mrs Daltry snatched Ricky's cap off his head.

"Don't wear this in the classroom, Ricky. I've told you that before," she snapped, waving the cap above Ricky's head.

"Sorry, Mrs Daltry," Ricky muttered. "Can I have it back?"

"No. I'll return it at the end of the day," Mrs Daltry said tartly. She shoved Ricky's cap into her jacket pocket.

Angela leaned against the wall in the corridor, watching. She waited until Mrs Daltry strode by them, chewing on yet another liquorice allsort, before speaking.

"Theo, you're not allowed to tell anyone your dare," Angela said urgently. "That goes for you too, Ricky."

"You didn't have to wait behind to tell us that. We know the rules," Ricky frowned.

"Yeah, you've told us often enough." Theo sniffed resentfully.

Who did Angela think she was – staying behind to show them up like that? Did she think they were going to cheat the moment her back was turned?

"Just saying," Angela replied. And with that, off she marched.

Theo took a look at Ricky. Ricky looked how Theo felt – annoyed!

"Never mind her. She's just a weevil head and three-quarters," Ricky said.

"A weevil head and seven-eighths."

"A weevil head and fifteen-sixteenths."

Ricky and Theo made their way to the lunch hall. By that time Angela was a weevil head and two hundred and fifty-five, two hundred and fifty-sixths!

Theo felt horrible. More horrible than he'd ever felt in his life before. Dad placed a hand on Theo's forehead, tutting over and over as he did so.

"You are burning up," said Dad.

"Bu' I feezin'," Theo protested.

"What was that?" Dad took the thermometer out of Theo's mouth.

"But I'm freezing," Theo repeated. "And

everything aches. And my headache's getting worse. And I feel like this tissue here." Theo held up a tissue which he'd only used twice and already it was on its last legs – soggy and falling apart!

"A few days in bed and you'll be back to your normal gungy, grungy self," said Dad.

"But I can't stay in bed…"

"Theo, you've got the flu and moaning about it won't change it," Dad interrupted, popping the thermometer back into Theo's mouth.

Theo groaned. What about his dare? What about his twenty-five pounds? It wasn't fair. It was all Mrs Daltry's fault. She was the one who'd sent for Dad after the afternoon break. Theo was sure he could've made it to the end of the day but his teacher disagreed.

"You look terrible, you sound worse and I'm not going to let you pass your germs on to everyone else in the class," Mrs Daltry had told him testily. "You're going home."

Ordinarily, Theo would've been glad to go home. But not today of all days. Now Mum and Dad would be watching him like a hawk. How would he ever get out of the house to get to 117 Buzan Road for midnight? Theo took the thermometer out of his mouth.

"Dad… I don't suppose you and Mum will let me go out this evening – just for an hour?" Theo asked.

Dad stared at Theo. "You must be crazy out of your head! You're not going anywhere tonight."

Theo sighed. He had his answer. The doorbell rang.

"And keep that thermometer in your mouth," Dad ordered. "I'll be right back."

Dad left the room, still muttering incredulously at Theo's request. Theo twisted and turned in his bed, trying to get comfortable. He pulled his duvet up past his neck. He was freezing, and yet perspiration was dripping off him like rainwater. He'd never felt so lousy. It felt like every drop of blood in his body was hurting. And he was going to lose the dare contest. That was what hurt the most.

A minute later, Theo's bedroom door

opened. The peak of a baseball cap appeared first, followed by Ricky's head.

"Can I come in?" he asked softly.

Theo took the thermometer out of his mouth. "If you don't mind catching my germs," he sniffed, reaching for yet another tissue from his bedside table.

Ricky walked into the room, carefully closing the door behind him.

"Your dad said I can't stay long," Ricky whispered.

Theo frowned and struggled to sit up.

"Ricky, why're you whispering?"

"Am I?" Ricky's voice was even quieter than before.

Theo raised his eyebrows. Ricky laughed.

"Sorry," Ricky said ruefully, his voice back to normal. "How're you feeling?"

"Like a plate of week-old spaghetti," Theo replied. "Ricky, I'm in trouble. What am I going to do about my dare? I was meant to do it tonight."

"Can't you put it off until tomorrow or some time later this week?"

"No. It's got to be tonight or never. I'm meant to go somewhere later and I feel terrible. Besides, there's no way Mum and Dad will let me get past the front door. If it wasn't for this rotten cold, I'd have won the twenty-five pounds for sure," Theo said glumly.

"You reckon? You're sicker than I thought!" Ricky replied. "It's affecting your brain!"

"I'm too ill to argue with you." Theo reached out for another tissue. He had another coughing fit, followed by one sneeze after another after another. After that, Theo collapsed back against his pillows.

"You sound like a frog on a bad day and look like year-old spaghetti, not week-old spaghetti," Ricky said, with his version of sympathy.

Theo nodded. "I know." He wiped his nose. "So what was your dare like? Have you done it yet?"

Ricky shook his head. "Just thinking about it makes me want to chuck!"

"Is it really that sick-making?" Theo asked.

Ricky nodded, his face long. Theo and Ricky watched each other. Theo was dying to know what Ricky's dare was. And from the look on Ricky's face, he was thinking the same thing. Suddenly Ricky stared at Theo, his eyes huge and bright. A slow smile crept over his face.

"I've got it!" He waved his hands in the air.

"Got what?"

"The perfect solution." Ricky grinned. "Your dare has to be done tonight and mine doesn't. So why don't we swap dares?"

"Swap? But Angela said—"

"If you don't tell her, I won't," Ricky interrupted. "Come on. If we keep it to ourselves, who's to know?"

"Isn't it cheating?"

"No. All we're doing is swapping. I won't help you with yours and you won't help me with mine," Ricky replied. He had it all figured out.

"What's your dare?" Theo asked suspiciously.

"Oh, no, you don't," Ricky said. "If you agree then we swap dares and we don't swap back."

"Can't I see it first? It might be worse than the one I've already got," Theo argued.

"You can't leave your house to do the one you've got, so what difference does it make?" Ricky pointed out.

Theo thought for a moment. "And it's strictly between us two?"

"Yep!"

"Promise?"

"Promise."

"Oh, all right then. Hand your dare over."

Ricky fished into his jacket pocket and took out a now crumpled piece of paper.

"Where's your one?" he asked.

Theo lifted up his pillow and took out his dare. Ricky walked over to Theo. He tentatively held out his piece of paper. Theo did the same. Their hands were about twenty centimetres apart but neither of them moved closer.

"After three?" Ricky suggested.

Theo nodded.

"One…"

"Two…"

"*Three!*"

They each grabbed for the piece of paper in the other's hand. His heart hammering, Theo smoothed out Ricky's crumpled piece of paper.

You will ask Sarah McWilliam out for a date. You must take her for a meal or to the pictures before the end of next week – your treat!

Theo stared in total horror. Sarah! The worst girl in the class! The worst girl in the whole school! It was bad enough that she sat behind him and was constantly tap-tapping on his shoulder, but now he had to take her out as well? Not a chance! Not in this lifetime!

"I want my old dare back," Theo said immediately.

"No way!" Ricky laughed. "We made a deal."

"I'm not taking Sarah out anywhere. I'd rather eat one of Mum's fish pies. I'd rather mow the lawn for the next ten years. I'd rather have the flu for the next one hundred years!" Theo shook his head so hard, his neck started hurting.

"Tough!" Ricky grinned. He looked down at the dare in his hand. "This is easy compared to taking Sarah out! I'll have to sneak out of our flat but that's no problem. I'll wear my action man kit – trainers, black jeans, black jacket, black baseball cap... It'll be fun!"

"Stuff fun! Give me my old dare back," Theo demanded.

"Not a chance."

"*Please!*"

Ricky shook his head, not even trying to hide the victorious smirk on his face.

"But Sarah probably wrote this herself!" Theo tossed the dare aside as if the paper were suddenly burning his fingers.

"Tough and two-thirds!" Ricky replied.

Dad came into the room with a glass of orange juice.

"I think that's enough for this evening, Ricky. Theo needs his rest," said Dad.

"Okay, Mr Mosley," Ricky said. "I was just going anyway."

Ricky practically sprinted to the bedroom door. "See you tomorrow, Theo," he smiled.

"Ricky…"

Theo attempted to get out of bed. Too late! Ricky was gone. Moments later, Theo heard the front door slam shut.

"Where d'you think you're going?" Dad asked. "Back in bed."

Reluctantly, Theo swung his legs back between the sheets.

"Mum'll be home soon," Dad smiled as he tucked Theo in, before sitting down at the edge of the bed. Then he spotted the thermometer on the duvet.

"Oh, yeah! I forgot about that," Dad said, popping it back in Theo's mouth. His smile turned into a sudden grimace and he groaned. "I've just had a horrible thought. As you're ill, Mum'll probably insist on doing one of her fish pies for dinner. Why does she always wait until one of us is sick before inflicting it on us?"

"Some form of torture so we'll hurry up and get well?" Theo suggested grimly, before putting the thermometer back into his mouth.

"Or maybe she reckons that's the only time we'll eat it, when we're too weak to argue," said Dad.

Dad and Theo grimaced at each other in total sympathy.

Theo sagged back against his pillows. What had he done to deserve Sarah *and* Mum's fish pie, all in the one day? Being sick was the pits!

4 I DID IT...

19:00hrs Thursday, 15th May

Well, I did it. Theo will be at the warehouse at midnight tonight and I'll be watching. He'll be all right – I hope. Please God, let him be all right. Please don't let anything go wrong. Don't let him get caught...

5 RICKY DISAPPEARS

Theo took a deep breath, held it and pressed the button to take one more step. He died instantly! A huge snake's head appeared on the screen and grinned maliciously at him. Theo hated the way the snakes always grinned at you when you stepped on them. But at least he didn't have to listen to the snake sniggering at him because the telly volume was turned right down.

"Stupid game anyway," he muttered to himself.

Theo went over to the games console and took out "Rattlesnake", which at that moment was one of his least favourite games! Then he went through all his other games cartridges. What should he play next? It would've been great if Ricky was there to play the games with him. Playing by yourself got a bit tedious after a while. Never mind, Ricky was bound to come and see him after school.

"Theo, I hope you're resting in there."

"Yes, Mum," Theo called back.

He'd had a real battle persuading Mum to allow him downstairs. He'd been in bed all morning and most of the afternoon but Mum seemed to think he should stay put, remain still and not even blink unless it was absolutely vital. Theo'd grumbled on and on for so long that Mum finally let him come downstairs just to shut him up. But she insisted that he kept a blanket wrapped around him and stayed put on the sofa.

"No telly. No CDs. Read a book or sleep," Mum ordered.

That was why the volume on the telly was turned right down. Mum'd taken the day off to stay with him, but she was still working from her PC in the front room. Theo didn't want to disturb her – that way she wouldn't find out he was playing video games!

Theo had decided that he'd play "Time-trip" next, when the doorbell rang. He glanced at the LED display on the video recorder. Who on earth could be calling at half past three in the afternoon? He went out into the hall as Mum opened the door.

It was the police – a tall, black man and a woman with brown hair, both in uniform. And Mrs Burridge, Ricky's mum.

Theo stared. The police… They hadn't yet said a word and already his heart was beginning to thump in an odd, hiccupy way. And Ricky's mum – she looked terrible. There were dark rings around her glistening eyes, her lips were a thin, pinched line and her hands circled each other constantly. Her eyes darted back and forth, taking in every part of the hall as if searching for something.

"Mrs Mosley?" the policeman enquired.

"Ricky? RICKY?" Ricky's mum called out at the top of her voice.

Theo's mum switched her puzzled gaze

from the police to Ricky's mum. "Etta, Ricky's not here. What's wrong? What's the matter?"

Ricky's mum's eyes filled with tears which spilt over on to her cheeks.

"Ricky…" she began hoarsely. "Ricky's disappeared. He's gone missing."

Theo gasped, winded as if he'd been kicked in the stomach.

"What d'you mean – he's gone missing?" Theo's mum asked, shocked. "Look, come in. Come in all of you."

Mum led the way to the living-room. Theo stepped out of the way but the grown-ups were all too preoccupied to take any notice of him.

"We understand that Ricky arrived home safely after visiting Theo last night but…" The policeman didn't get any further.

"We both had a late supper, then watched telly. He was supposed to go to bed after that, but this morning I found that his bed hadn't been slept in. I … I don't know what to do." Ricky's mum kept clenching and unclenching her hands – over and over. As if suddenly aware of what her hands were doing, she hugged her arms tightly about herself before speaking again. "Are you certain Ricky isn't here? I was hoping…"

"Oh, Etta, I'm so sorry. We haven't seen him since he left yesterday evening," Theo's mum said. "I wish we had."

"Oh. I see. Are … are you sure?"

Theo's mum nodded unhappily. "I'm sure there's a perfectly reasonable explanation for all this. Ricky will turn up soon, I'm sure he will."

"Yes, of course he will," Ricky's mum agreed, her voice barely audible.

Theo's mum put her arm around Ricky's mum's shoulders. Neither of them spoke. A tangible fear descended on the room. Theo swallowed hard, then swallowed again. Fear clogged his throat. Ricky… The policeman and woman exchanged a look, their faces sombre.

"Theo, we understand that you and Ricky are very good friends. Did he say anything to you about going somewhere late last night or this morning?" asked the policeman.

Theo was burning up – from the top of his head to the tips of his toenails. And he couldn't breathe. No matter how hard he tried, he just couldn't catch his breath.

"It's all right, Theo. Don't be afraid," said the policeman. "I'm sure we'll find Ricky safe and sound."

Theo gasped audibly. He still couldn't get his breath. It was as if he was underwater, fighting to find a way up and out, fighting not to drown. Ricky was missing.

Ricky was missing…

Was it the dare? It couldn't be the dare. It'd been so simple. A matter of spending an hour after midnight crouched in the ventilator shaft of a warehouse behind the precinct. Nothing spiteful. Nothing dangerous… But maybe the ventilator shaft had collapsed. Maybe the whole building had collapsed. What if Ricky was trapped, or hurt, or worse…

"Theo?"

Theo turned his stricken gaze to his mum.

"Theo, d'you know where Ricky is?" Mum asked slowly.

Theo's tongue was frozen to the roof of his mouth and it refused to budge.

"Theo?" his mum prompted softly.

The dare contest. They weren't meant to tell anyone about it. But Ricky... Where was Ricky? Theo swallowed hard.

"117 Buzan Road. The warehouse." Theo's breath came out in a desperate rush.

None of the grown-ups spoke.

"It was a dare." Theo fought to keep his voice steady. "Ricky had to spend an hour at 117 Buzan Road from midnight last night."

"A dare?" Ricky's mum asked, sharply. "You dared him?"

"NO! No. It's a game and practically everyone in our class is playing. He didn't get my dare." Theo shook his head. He couldn't get his head clear. His words were coming out in a horribly confused jumble, but in spite of that, the grown-ups seemed to understand him.

"And Ricky was dared to go to 117 Buzan

Road?" The policewoman frowned.

Theo nodded, his left hand cupped inside his right to hide the fact that he was crossing his fingers. He was seconds away from being sick – actually being sick on the living-room carpet. If Ricky was hurt or trapped then it'd be all his fault.

Because the dare had originally been his...

"I'll radio in this new information," said the policeman.

He took out his radio and walked into the hall.

"Mrs Burridge, I don't suppose we can persuade you to go home and wait for us to call you?" the policewoman asked.

"No. I'm coming with you," Ricky's mum argued. "If you don't take me, I'll run all the way there if I have to."

"Calm down, Mrs Burridge. We'll take you," the policewoman soothed.

The policeman came back into the room. "Well, there's been nothing untoward reported from Buzan Road in the last twenty-four hours, but we'll check it out anyway."

"Etta, let me know … what happens…"
Theo's mum struggled to find the right words.

Ricky's mum nodded.

"We may need to come back to get more information from Theo," the policeman warned.

"I understand," said Theo's mum.

She escorted them to the front door and let them out. Theo watched, afraid to blink or move in case he missed something. He felt so strange. So peculiar. So *calm*. But it wasn't real. It was as if there was a storm raging all around him and slowly but surely closing in on him.

The moment the front door was shut, Theo's mum turned to face him, her eyes filled with worry and concern and the anger that sprang from both.

"Right, young man. I want to know all about this dare business and exactly what you've been up to," she demanded.

And the storm descended.

6 AN OMISSION AND A FIND

On Monday morning, the weather was horrible. The weatherman on the radio had called it a "marvellous Mediterranean scorcher". As far as Theo was concerned it was hot and sticky and it wasn't even eight-thirty yet. It would make what he had to do that much more difficult.

"Theo, are you sure you're able to go to school?" Mum asked.

"That's the umpteenth and a half time you've asked me that," Theo said. "I'm fine."

"You sure you're over the flu?" Dad frowned.

"'Course! I'm super fit," Theo smiled. "I've only got a little bit of a sniffle left."

"Hhmm!" Mum wasn't convinced.

"Hhmm!" Neither was Dad!

"I wouldn't be going to school if I didn't feel OK," Theo pointed out.

"Hhhmmm! I guess not. You know you can stay home for another day if you want to." Theo's mum still wasn't completely satisfied.

Theo forced his smile to widen. "No, thanks."

"Are you sure?"

"Mum, Dad – chill!" Theo said, exasperated. "What's this meant to be? Nagging in stereo?"

"We're only asking…"

"I want to know why you're in such a rush to get to school." Dad raised an eyebrow.

"Because I'm fine," Theo said firmly.

He'd never had to act so hard in his life. His head was pounding and his body still ached, and as for "a little bit of a sniffle" – it was more like the river Thames running through his nose! But he knew there was no way Mum and Dad would let him out of the house unless he convinced them that he'd got over his flu.

And he had to get out of the house.

Because Ricky was still missing.

Ricky's mum had phoned late on Friday night to tell them that Ricky hadn't been found and that the police had found 117 Buzan Road empty and deserted. She hadn't phoned back since to say otherwise. On Sunday evening, Dad phoned the police who told him that they were stepping up the search for Ricky. Dad asked again about the warehouse on Buzan Road. As far as the police were concerned there was no sign that Ricky had ever been near the place.

But Theo felt there had to be more to it than that – the sick, anxious feeling in the pit of his stomach told him so. Ricky's disappearance had something to do with the dare – Theo was sure of it. Now it was up to him to find Ricky and prove it. He'd already lost the weekend because Mum and Dad wouldn't let him out of the house. There was no way he was going to lose yet another day. He'd lost too much time already. He had to find Ricky – he just had to.

"See you later, Mum. 'Bye, Dad." Theo fled out of the house before his parents could say another word.

He glanced down at his watch. He'd have to hurry if he was going to make it to Buzan Road before school started.

117 Buzan Road was a huge, two-storey warehouse with dirty-grey, barred windows and a heavily padlocked front entrance. The roof was flat and the whole building looked what it was, derelict and neglected. Theo stood outside the front doors. He wiped the perspiration from his forehead, wondering vaguely if it was the weather or the flu or what he might find that was causing him to sweat so much. Theo looked around. How could he get past the front gates for a closer look? Had the police got into the warehouse? They must've done. They'd probably contacted the warehouse owner, got the keys and walked in. Theo would have to find another way.

"Come on, Theo – think!" he told himself sternly.

How would Ricky have got in?

"Of course!" Theo mentally kicked himself. *The ventilator shaft!*

Theo turned and walked to his right, scrutinizing the building for the ventilator shaft mentioned in the dare. Nothing. Surreptitiously, Theo looked around again. He wanted to make sure he wasn't being watched. No, he was safe. Everyone was in a hurry, their eyes on the road straight ahead as they rushed to work or school. Theo ducked around the side of the building. Was the ventilator shaft here? He carried on walking and searching. Still nothing. And he couldn't get round the back because a big double gate blocked his way.

The entrance to the shaft had to be round the other side of the building. Blowing his nose, Theo strolled out on to the main road, fervently hoping that he didn't look suspicious. The last thing he wanted was to attract attention. He walked past the front entrance, still searching for the elusive ventilator shaft. He turned round the corner and searched along the other side of the building. Eureka! There it was! A half-metre high mesh grille in front of the ventilator shaft.

Theo took a quick look around again. It was all clear. He crouched down.

"Ricky?" Theo whispered through the grille. Silence. "Ricky?" He tried again, louder this time.

Theo ran his fingers along the top of the grille, then down the sides, looking for a gap into which he could work his fingers to pull the whole grille off. Nothing doing. The grille was tight against the wall. Theo sat back on his heels and frowned. Something wasn't right... Something was *missing*. Then Theo realized what it was. Dust! There was no dust on his fingers. There was no dust on the grille. That proved that Ricky had found a way to move the grille and the dust had fallen off it. Or maybe the dust had fallen off when the police moved it — if they had...

Theo's eyes widened with shock as he realized something else. He *hadn't* told the police about the ventilator shaft. Theo frowned deeply as he tried to remember just what he *had* said. He'd told them about the dares and the address of the warehouse but not about the ventilator shaft – he was sure of it.

"RICKY?" Theo called urgently through the mesh.

Even if the police had searched the warehouse, they might still have missed Ricky if he was injured in this shaft somewhere. Theo swallowed hard, the sick feeling in the pit of his stomach intensifying. Lacing his fingers into the holes in the mesh, Theo pulled as hard as he could. He winced as the wire mesh cut deeply into his fingers, but he didn't stop. One corner of the grille shifted. Theo pulled harder. Suddenly, unexpectedly, the grille came right away from the wall. Theo fell over backwards, hitting the ground with a hard THUMP! Quickly he looked around. It was all right, he was still alone.

Theo sat upright and peered into the shaft. After about a metre, it melted into darkness. Theo knelt closer.

"Ricky…" His voice was a whisper again.

A bird rose from his stomach to flutter in his throat – at least that's what it felt like. He didn't fancy going into the shaft at all, but if Ricky had gone in there then he had to too. He had to find out what'd happened to his friend. Theo glanced down at his watch. He'd have to hurry, or he'd be late for school.

Taking a deep breath, Theo crawled into the shaft. It was filthy-dirty and full of dust which made him sneeze – and the stink! It was like diesel fumes and cigarette smoke and rabbit, mouse and elephant droppings all mixed up into a noxious cocktail. The smell whistled up his nose like a sharp wind, in spite of his cold.

The floor was littered with bits of dirt and debris, some too small to see in the half light of the tunnel but not too small to dig into his palms and knees and shins as he moved forwards. But that wasn't the thing that slowed him down. No, what made him hesitate was the darkness sweeping over him like a slow tide, in spite of the bright sunlight outside. The light in the shaft was a darkening grey with swirls of dust like a mist dancing all around him. Theo crawled on, waving his hand before him every so often in a vain attempt to keep the dust out of his eyes and nose. And the tunnel grew narrower as he crawled on, until he had to tuck his head and elbows in to make sure he didn't hit the top or the sides of the tunnel.

After crawling what felt like half the length of a football pitch, the shaft split into three, with tunnels to the left and right as well as straight ahead. Theo looked down each tunnel in turn. Each one looked like the others. Theo dug out a tissue and wiped his nose as he considered. Straight ahead. He'd try the tunnel straight ahead first. He carried on crawling.

Minutes passed. Theo's back was beginning to ache from being hunched up for so long. He longed to stand up straight and stretch out but it wasn't possible, not in that narrow shaft. Theo was beginning to think about maybe turning back when he saw a strange light ahead. He moved faster, his eyes still on the light. His right hand landed on something soft – like material. Instantly, Theo drew his hand away in case it was something yucky! It was a black baseball cap. Theo snatched it up and turned it over. "CHILL!" was written across the front. Ricky's cap... There was no doubt about it. A shock, like summer lightning, flashed through Theo's body.

Ricky *was* here. In this shaft.

"RICKY!" Theo hollered at the top of his voice. "ARE YOU IN HERE?"

Silence. Dust swirled madly around him, but nothing else stirred. Theo took up Ricky's cap and stuffed it into his trouser pocket. He moved towards the light in front of him. At last he could see where it was coming from – grimy windows up and down the opposite wall, flooding the deserted warehouse floor with an eerie blue-yellow light. And from Theo's position he could see that the warehouse was deserted.

Theo sighed with disappointment. He sat for a few moments, frustration washing over him.

But what did he expect? The police had already been here and they hadn't found Ricky.

But they hadn't known about the ventilator shaft. So Ricky could still be in one of the tunnels somewhere. Theo tried to turn around to go back the way he came. He couldn't. The tunnel was too narrow. Panic, like a sneeze, began to tickle at him.

"Don't you dare," Theo muttered sternly. "Don't you dare lose your head and panic and flip and lose your cool and be a doof and … and let Ricky down."

The last one seemed to do the trick! Then all at once, Theo realized what he had to do. He started crawling backwards. Each second seemed to last for ever as Theo made his slow, careful way backwards through the tunnel. It took twice as long as before. The dust was worse, swirling and spinning up into his mouth and nose and eyes. And it was getting unbearably hot. His chest was tight and his head was beginning to hurt, but Theo couldn't give up. Not now. Not yet. Ricky might need him.

At last Theo reached the place where the shaft branched off in three directions. Here at last he could turn around. Now it wasn't so bad. But even so, Theo wanted to leave, to get out into the open and breathe air that wasn't full of dust and dirt. He looked ahead longingly, then turned and crawled along the tunnel to his left. This tunnel also ended with a grille looking out over a warehouse floor, but to Theo's surprise, it looked out over the darkened basement level rather than the ground floor. The ceiling was a couple of metres above him, whilst the floor was three metres below. Theo backed up and tried the only tunnel he hadn't yet explored. This one just led to another part of the ground floor. There was no further sign of Ricky. Theo didn't know whether to be sad or grateful. But not finding Ricky unconscious in the shaft meant that Ricky was all right. Ricky was safe … *wasn't he?*

Theo couldn't leave the ventilator shaft fast enough. He emerged from it, coughing and spluttering, his mouth full of goodness only knew what. After the shaft, the sunlight was warm and welcome.

"I'm not going in there again," Theo muttered.

And he certainly wasn't. Not if he could possibly help it. He glanced down at his watch, then stared.

Nine-thirty!

How did it get so late already? Theo took off up the street, oblivious to the startled looks being directed at him. Mrs Daltry was going to bite off his head and play football with it!

7 SOMEONE'S LYING

Theo took a deep breath, then another.

Might as well get it over with, he thought.

He opened his classroom door, his eyes on the ground. He didn't want to watch Mrs Daltry winding up for attack. He'd seen it plenty of times before.

But the attack never came. The room was totally silent. Theo looked up and immediately his breath caught in his throat.

Two policemen stood in the room, at the front of the class. One of the policemen was stocky, the other was beansprout thin.

"You've found Ricky?" Theo asked eagerly.

"No, they haven't. And where on earth have

you been? You're covered in dust. No, never mind. Just hurry up and sit down," Mrs Daltry said in a rush.

"You're Theo Mosley, is that right?" asked the stocky policeman.

Theo nodded. He looked around. All eyes were on him.

"Theo?" Mrs Daltry prompted impatiently.

Theo stumbled to his desk and plonked himself down. The chair next to him seemed ominously empty. Ricky's chair… Theo tore his eyes away from it. Why were the police here? Why weren't they out looking for Ricky?

"Now we know from Theo that some of you were playing a dare game. How many of you were playing?" the stocky policeman asked, his tone light and friendly.

Theo's face started to burn. What would everyone else think about him telling the police about the dare game? Theo straightened up in his chair, his lips set. It didn't matter what everyone else thought. Ricky was more important than some stupid game. It was just tough and three-quarters if the others didn't like it.

"It's all right, I promise. We just want to know how many of you were involved in this game?" The stocky policeman smiled. He was the only one of the two policemen doing any talking.

Reluctantly, hands started going up into the air.

Both policemen looked around the room slowly. The policeman who seemed to be in charge turned his attention to Theo. "Theo, what was Ricky's dare? Try to remember."

Theo swallowed hard. "It said something like – 'At midnight, enter the deserted warehouse at 117 Buzan Road, behind the shopping precinct. Go into the ventilation shaft, wait for an hour until 1 a.m., then leave. If you don't stay for the full hour, you lose.' Something like that."

"Oh, so the dares were written down?" the policeman said, surprised.

Theo nodded. "We all had to write down anonymous dares and put them in a carrier bag.

Then we each got a dare which we had to do."

"So who wrote down Ricky's dare?" asked the policeman.

All the hands came down. Theo looked around. He'd been wondering that himself. The hands stayed down. Then Theo remembered something else. He put his hand up.

"Yes, Theo?" Mrs Daltry prompted.

"I've just remembered what Ricky's dare had written at the end of it," said Theo. "It said, 'I'll be watching.'"

Silence. The classroom was as still as a cemetery at night for a few moments. It was as if everyone in the room was holding their breath.

"Let me say again that we're not interested in blaming anyone or getting anyone into trouble," said the stocky policeman. "At this stage we just want to find Ricky. So please, who wrote that dare?"

Theo looked around again. No one moved.

The policeman in charge walked over to Mrs Daltry and they muttered together for a few moments. Theo strained closer to hear what they were saying, as did everyone else, but the words were indistinct.

Mrs Daltry shook her head, then pointed to the whiteboards at the front and side of the classroom. The policeman reluctantly nodded before turning around.

"We'd like each of you in turn to write out the dares you made up last week," the policeman explained. "And please initial your dare once you've written it down."

Theo risked a curious glance at the skinny policeman. He still hadn't said a word and it didn't look like he was going to either. Was he just there to watch – to see if anyone gave themselves away?

"Claire and Robert, you can start," Mrs Daltry said, handing out blue pens to the two pupils closest to her.

Robert and Claire rose unwillingly to their feet. They walked over to the whiteboards, their arms lying like wet socks at their sides.

"Well?" Mrs Daltry prompted.

Hesitantly, they both started to write.

"If you're a boy, I dare you to wear a frilly

dress and walk around the block in it. You must be seen by at least one other person in the class or it doesn't count. If you're a girl, I dare you to get one of the boys in the class to wear a frilly dress and walk around the block without telling him why," Claire wrote.

"So that was *you* was it, you bat-breathed dweeb? I got that one!" Tony said with disgust.

Everyone creased up laughing. Theo read Claire's dare enviously. He wished he'd thought of that one!

"That's enough," Mrs Daltry said sternly. "All of you just remember Ricky and why we're doing this."

The laughter died away instantly.

"Write a letter asking Mrs McMurtry if she's bald under her wig and sign it." Robert's writing got smaller and smaller towards the end of the sentence, but not small enough! It could still be read, even from the back of the class.

Everyone reckoned the headmistress, Mrs McMurtry, was as bald as an egg because of the funny-peculiar way her hair sat on her head. No one would deliberately style their hair like that, so it had to be a wig – at least, that was the consensus. Mrs Daltry tutted heavily but didn't comment on either of the dares.

"OK, leave the pens up there and sit down," she ordered. "Chris, Danny, you're next."

One by one, everyone had to go up to the front of the class and write down their dares. Theo'd been right about the dare Ricky had swapped with him. Sarah *had* written it herself!

She must've reckoned that even if a girl got her dare, she'd still get to eat and see a film for free, Theo thought with disgust.

Many minutes passed before the last dare was written down. Both whiteboards were covered from top to bottom with scribbled dares. And not one of them mentioned Buzan Road or being there at midnight. Angry, Theo looked around the room again. Some-one was lying.

"Theo, you're sure about what was written on Ricky's dare?" asked the stocky policeman doubtfully.

"Positive," Theo replied. "That's what it said, I promise."

The grown-ups turned around to read the dares again.

"Someone didn't write down their real dare." Theo voiced his thoughts.

"Right then. I'd like each of you to come up here in turn and write your name next to the dare you *received*. Not the one you wrote, the one you got," said the policeman.

Theo understood at once. The person who'd lied and written down a brand new dare would be found out when no one claimed their dare. Clever! He looked quickly around the class. No one looked particularly anxious or upset – at least, not as far as he could see.

"The dare I got isn't on the board," Janice complained.

"Then we'll assume your dare was written by Ricky," the policeman smiled.

Five minutes later, every dare had the writer's initials and the receiver's name next to it. Theo sat back, puzzled. He couldn't understand it – unless there were *two* people lying? But that couldn't be right. No, Ricky's dare had been written by someone working alone – Theo was sure of it. But then, how come each dare had a name written next to it? There weren't any left over. Unless...

"Could those people who received the dares they wrote themselves please put their hands up," said the policeman lightly.

That was just what Theo was thinking. If he'd written out a new dare to cover his tracks, he'd have no choice now but to claim it as the one he'd also picked out. And he was sure that was just what the person who was lying had done.

As Theo looked around, three people put their hands up. Colin, Angela and Shirley...

"Hhmm! I see."

The two policemen turned their backs on the class and whispered together.

When the policeman in charge turned back

to the class, he said, "You can put your hands down now."

Angela's arm was already at her side. Colin and Shirley put their hands down.

"I think all I'd say at this juncture is if any of you see or hear from Ricky or remember anything, anything at all that could help us, please phone the police or get your parents to phone us," said the policeman.

"Is that it? Is that all you're going to do? Someone's *lying*…" Theo protested.

"Theo, that's enough," Mrs Daltry admonished.

The policeman opened his mouth to speak, then closed it, looking thoughtful.

"I'd also like to say this." He waved his hand in the direction of the two whiteboards. "Playing so-called games for money can be very dangerous. I see that none of these dares is out-and-out dangerous but a lot of them are … dubious, to say the least. And apart from anything else, you might start out as friends playing these kinds of games for money, but that's not how you'd end up – I guarantee it.

It's not worth it. So my advice is – don't do it. And consider the consequences. Ricky Burridge is *missing*…"

"Thank you, Sergeant Ridley. I'm sure we've all heard and understood every word you've said." Mrs Daltry looked around the room slowly, her blazing eyes sending laser bolts into anyone brave enough to return her gaze. Looking at her, Theo was sure that none of them had heard the last of this dare business.

"We have to go now. We have other classrooms to visit," said the stocky policeman. "But if anyone remembers anything that might help find Ricky, get in touch with us. It's very important that you do."

As Mrs Daltry saw the two policemen to the door, Theo took out Ricky's crumpled-up cap from his trouser pocket and laid it on his lap beneath his table. He looked down at it.

"Ricky, where *are* you?" he mouthed to the cap.

A strange tingling appeared at the back of his neck. Theo rubbed his nape impatiently.

Then he realized what it meant. His head whipped around. Angela was watching him. The moment he caught her gaze, she looked away. Theo glared at her. She probably hated him for spoiling her dare game. Tough and fifteen-sixteenths! What did she want him to do? Say nothing to the police?

The moment the door closed behind the policemen, Mrs Daltry turned to the class.

"We all have some very serious talking to do," said Mrs Daltry. "Or rather I have some talking to do, you lot will listen…"

The mid-morning buzzer sounded. The whole class gave a collective sigh of relief.

"This isn't over yet. I want to see each and every one of you back here as soon as the break is over," said Mrs Daltry.

And she left the classroom. Theo could tell she was more than upset because she didn't pop a liquorice allsort into her mouth. Everyone else trooped out of the classroom after her, very subdued. Everyone except Theo.

He walked over to the whiteboards and examined every dare in turn. The dare he was after might not be on the board but what about the handwriting? Theo studied each written dare twice, then three and four times. It was no use. There were at least ten very likely samples of handwriting and at least another five possibles. Huffing with frustration, Theo dug his hands in his pockets. What should he do now?

Of course writing on a board was different from writing on a piece of paper. Except how would he get to see samples of everyone's handwriting as written on paper? And what about Ricky's cap? Should Theo hand it over to the police or not?

Soon, Theo decided. Very soon – but not now.

Theo still needed the cap. It was his only way of keeping close to Ricky.

8 WRONG

I'm sitting in the loos writing this. The smudges on the paper are from where I've been crying. I cry all the time now. The least little thing sets me off. I feel all alone and so frightened. It all went wrong. As wrong as can be. Tom guessed that it was all my fault. He told me not to tell the others – under any circumstances. I must never tell anyone. That's what he says.

Robbie is madder than a kicked dog about it and is ranting non-stop. Scott says nothing. Somehow that's worse. I've caught him giving me strange looks, but he hasn't said a word – at least, not directly to me.

Does he suspect me? From the way he keeps looking at me, he must do. But Ricky can't have told them yet that he and I go to the same school – otherwise Scott and Robbie would've said or done something by now. Ricky doesn't … shouldn't know I'm involved in this. He doesn't know about Tom being my brother, so maybe I'll get away with it. Maybe. If, as Tom says, I keep my mouth shut. Tom says if anything happens, he can handle the others. But he's just fooling himself. He wouldn't stand a chance against Robbie, and Scott's the sort to stab him in the back – literally. Dylan's a complete waste of space, so he wouldn't help. Dylan couldn't help himself out of the shallow end of a swimming pool.

I can't stop thinking about Ricky. I wish I could, but I can't. It's not my fault Ricky got caught up in the middle of all this. It's not my fault Ricky got caught at all. Who told him to come prying and poking around and sticking his nose in where it wasn't wanted? That's not my fault. It has nothing to do with me.

They're going to do the job the day after tomorrow. Robbie keeps going on about how nothing and no one is going to stop them now. Not the police, not the army and certainly not some little snot-nosed kid – as he calls Ricky.

Tom says they didn't mean to hurt Ricky but they didn't have any choice. Just thinking about it make me feel sick. There's a solid lump of something hard and heavy sitting in my chest. It's there all the time now.

I think it's fear.

It's not fair. Ricky getting caught was his own stupid fault. I can't do anything to help him – I wish I could, but I can't. I… I…

I've got to sign off. I can't stop crying. I wish I could just freeze the world and everything in it – just until I'd had a chance to sit down and think. I'm so frightened.

When will I stop feeling so frightened all the time?

9 DON'T TELL

"THEO, SIT DOWN!" Mrs Daltry was close to going nuclear! Theo was driving her nuts!

Theo walked the long way round the class to get to his desk. He stopped abruptly at Shirley's table and snatched up her work book. Flicking disdainfully through the pages, Theo then held the book by its spine and turned it upside down.

"Mrs Daltry, Theo's grabbed my book. Tell him!" Shirley complained.

"Theo, I'm not going to warn you again. I don't know what's got into you this afternoon but I'm not going to stand for any more," Mrs Daltry thundered.

Theo dropped Shirley's work book back down on to the desk from a great height and swaggered back to his seat. On the way he caught sight of Angela, yawning again. Before her mouth was closed, he grabbed her work book and started looking through it. Angela sprang to her feet and tried to seize it back.

"Give me back my book, you toad!" Angela demanded.

"Make me," Theo scoffed.

"Theo, that does it. You can sit outside in the corridor for the rest of the lesson," Mrs Daltry ordered.

Slowly, Theo handed Angela her book back, his eyes never leaving her face.

"Serve you right!" Angela hissed.

Theo didn't reply. He walked around the back of the class, now taking the long way round to get to the door. He passed Colin's table and looked over his shoulder to see what Colin was writing in his work book. Colin turned his head and scowled at Theo.

"Yes?" he asked curtly.

"Nothing." Theo shrugged.

And he walked out of the classroom, feeling Mrs Daltry's furious eyes boring into his back. He was careful to close the door quietly behind him, not wanting to bring down any more of Mrs Daltry's wrath around his ears.

Relieved, Theo sagged against the wall. He'd done it! One way or another he'd seen the normal handwriting of everyone in the class. He'd managed to take a look at most people's work books during the lunch break when the classroom was deserted. But some people had put their work books in their shoulder bags and taken their bags to lunch with them. For those people, Theo'd had no choice but to devise a way of seeing their books before the day was out, without arousing anyone's suspicions as to what he was really doing.

So here he was, in trouble with Mrs Daltry, but at least now he knew who'd written his original dare. Theo shook his head as if to clear the doubts that were beginning to creep into his head. If he was right about who'd written the dare, then it didn't make any sense. He still couldn't figure out *why* they'd written it. So the only thing to do now was confront them and demand to know what had happened to Ricky.

Should I go to the police...? Theo wondered.

No. Not until he had some concrete proof. The police would never believe him otherwise. So first Theo had to find out what was going on. He'd get proof – and then he'd talk to the police. That made more sense.

The minutes dragged by until the buzzer sounded for the start of the afternoon break. Theo turned to face the door. He breathed deeply, trying to smooth out the knots in his stomach. He'd have to follow the person he suspected out of the school building and wait for a suitable moment before confronting them. It wouldn't be easy, but the more Theo thought about it, the more convinced he became that he was on the right track.

Mrs Daltry was the sixth or seventh out of the classroom. Theo peered past her, wondering where the person he was waiting for had got to.

"Theo, follow me," Mrs Daltry commanded.

"Pardon?"

"You'll be sitting outside the staff room this break time," said Mrs Daltry.

"Oh, but … but I've got things to do," Theo protested.

"Too bad. You waste my time, I waste yours – that's the way it works," said Mrs Daltry.

"But…"

"Keep arguing and you'll be outside the staff room during all the breaks for the rest of the week," Mrs Daltry warned.

Theo's mouth snapped shut.

"That's better," said Mrs Daltry. "Now follow me."

And Theo had no choice but to trail along beside his teacher as she strode down the corridor, surreptitiously popping a liquorice allsort into her mouth as she did so.

So much for his wonderful plan! It'd just have to wait until after school. He sighed impatiently, then again with total frustration. But there was nothing he could do except wait.

When they both reached the staff room, Mrs Daltry turned to Theo.

"I realize you're worried about Ricky, but that's no excuse for your behaviour today. You're usually so quiet and now I've seen the alternative, I want the old Theo back. Do I make myself clear?" asked the teacher.

Theo nodded.

"We're all worried about Ricky." Mrs Daltry rested a hand on Theo's shoulder. "You're Ricky's closest friend and I know how you must be feeling – that's why I'm not sending you to the headmistress." Mrs Daltry's arm dropped to her side. "But no more unruly behaviour – OK?"

"OK," Theo agreed. He didn't need to play about any more – he had what he wanted. "Can I go for my break now?"

"No. Cause and effect, Theo. Cause and effect."

Theo sighed. Cause and effect! Mrs Daltry's second favourite saying!

"You misbehaved, Theo and the effect is?" the teacher prompted.

"No break time," said Theo glumly.

Mrs Daltry shrugged. "You have to learn that life is not a bowl of cherries."

And there it was again – Mrs Daltry's favourite saying! Theo watched his teacher enter the staff room, popping yet another liquorice allsort into her mouth.

Theo sat miserably watching as the others in his class made their way past him on their way out into the sunshine. Colin frowned at him. Shirley glowered. Some others grinned. And then Angela came out of the classroom, her head bent as she tried to fasten her bag. She stumbled along the corridor, still fiddling with her bag. Her head snapped up as she suddenly became aware that she was being watched. Theo took a quick glance around, then leapt to his feet. Angela walked towards Theo, her head held high as she went to swan past him.

"I want to talk to you," Theo said.

"What makes you think it's mutual?" Angela sniffed.

She marched past Theo as if a particularly obnoxious smell had just developed under her nose.

Furious, Theo called after her, "Where's Ricky?"

Angela froze. Neither of them spoke. Theo didn't dare blink in case he missed something vital. Every word, every gesture, every move Angela made from now would be important. Theo's heart thump-thumped slowly in his chest. This was it. What if he was wrong…?

Angela turned slowly. "What d'you mean?" she frowned. "How should I know where Ricky is?"

"Because you're the one who made up his dare in the first place," Theo replied softly. "I saw the dare and I saw your handwriting in your work book. They were both exactly the same."

"I haven't a clue what you're talking about."

"You were watching that night. Just like you said you would in the dare. You know what happened to Ricky," Theo insisted.

"You're off your head…"

"Where is he?"

"I don't know."

"I don't believe you."

"That's your lookout."

They both spoke faster and faster, rushing out their accusations and denials. Everyone else in the school had ceased to exist as Angela and Theo verbally battled with each other.

"I said where's Ricky?" Theo demanded.

"And I said I don't know. I don't know anything about it," Angela replied harshly.

"Oh, no? You wrote Ricky's dare, I know you did."

"No, I didn't."

"You're a liar. We both know you're lying. Ricky's dare…"

"Shut up! Shut up about that stupid dare." Angela interrupted, her hands over her ears. "And it wasn't even Ricky's dare. It was yours and you…" Angela's mouth snapped shut.

Silence.

Theo stared at her. "So it *was* you," he breathed. "And you wanted *me* to disappear instead of Ricky."

"It wasn't like that."

"Why don't you tell Mrs Daltry and the police what it was like, then?" Theo replied furiously. "And if you don't, I will."

"No one will believe you." Desperation crept into Angela's voice.

"Yes, they will. I can prove you know where Ricky is."

"You're lying."

"You wanna bet?"

"I'll deny it."

"You can't. I... I..." Then Theo had a brainwave. "I've still got the original dare. The police can compare the handwriting. They'll know I'm telling the truth."

Angela stared at him, horror-stricken.

"Where's Ricky?" Theo's low voice rumbled like thunder.

"I don't know."

"WHERE'S RICKY?"

"*I don't know.*"

"I've had enough of this. If you won't tell me, you can tell the police." Theo marched over to the staff room door.

"Don't tell on me. You … you can't tell on me…" Angela whispered.

"Watch me." Theo raised his arm to knock on the door.

Angela moved like lightning to stop Theo's arm in mid flight.

"Don't," she pleaded. "If you tell Mrs Daltry or the police, they'll kill Ricky. They promised they would."

10 THE NEXT STEP

Stunned, Theo stared at Angela. Her eyes shimmered with unshed tears, her mouth quivered, she had trouble catching her breath. In that moment, Theo knew that she was telling the truth. She'd lied about other things – so many other things and he didn't understand everything that was going on, but in this, she was telling the truth.

"Who's going to kill Ricky?" Theo whispered.

"I ... I can't tell you."

"It's me or the police," Theo warned.

"Ricky heard and saw some things that he shouldn't have," Angela said miserably.

"Like what?"

"I can't say…" Angela began. "I really can't," she added desperately as Theo's hand once again reached out towards the staff room.

"D'you know where Ricky is?" Theo asked coldly.

Angela shook her head, brushing the back of one hand across her eyes.

"D'you at least know if he's all right?"

"Yes he is, I promise," Angela said eagerly.

"So what's going on?"

"I…"

Theo shook his head quickly. "And don't bother telling me that you can't tell me!"

Angela sighed but didn't speak.

"All right, then, answer this. Is Ricky being held against his will?" asked Theo.

Angela didn't reply.

"He must be – or he'd go home." Theo answered his own question. "We'd all have seen him by now."

Still Angela said nothing.

"Look, I'm sorry but I don't have any choice in this." Theo shook his head. "Ricky's being held somewhere against his will. I have to tell the police. If something bad were to happen to him, I'd never forgive myself."

"Nothing else will happen to Ricky, I promise. He'll be released soon, I'm sure of it."

"How can you be sure? You don't even know where he is," Theo said, exasperated. "I'm sorry, but I'm telling someone."

"*Please*. You don't understand. Ricky's safe for now." Angela looked down at the floor, unable to meet Theo's gaze. "Tom's looking out for him."

"Who's Tom?"

"My brother," Angela admitted. "That's why you can't tell the police. Tom will get into trouble if you do."

Theo and Angela watched each other silently. A few others in the corridor passed by, directing curious looks at them but neither Theo nor Angela saw them.

"What did I ever do to you?" Theo asked bitterly.

"I don't understand," Angela frowned.

"You gave your dare to me – deliberately passed it to me," Theo said with ice-cold fury. "*I* should be where Ricky is now. *I* should be the one being held against my will."

"I gave my dare to you because I thought you could help me. I th-thought you could tell me what Tom and the others are up to. It wasn't to set you up, I swear it wasn't. Why would I do that?" Angela asked, aghast.

"What made you think I could help you?"

"Because…" A slow blush crept up Angela's neck and across her cheeks. "Because you … you're quiet and quite small and I didn't think you'd get caught if you sneaked into the ventilator shaft at the warehouse. And … and I thought I could persuade you not to tell anyone but me what you found out."

"Oh, I see…" And Theo did see. He was the classroom mouse – scared of his own shadow. That was what everyone thought. Angela had only just joined the class and already she thought so too.

"You looked the most likely to help me. That was all there was to it," Angela said.

"Yeah, sure," Theo said resentfully.

"It's the truth."

Theo didn't reply. He turned his thoughts back to Ricky and this girl before him. He still wasn't sure of Angela and he certainly didn't trust her, but at that moment she was his only lead to his best friend. Theo leaned against the wall, still watching Angela. After a brief moment, she walked over to him and leaned against the wall beside him.

"Can you help me get to Ricky?" Theo asked softly. "I must see him. I want to make sure he's OK."

"I can try. I'll have to ask my brother where he is."

"Will he tell you?"

"I don't know," Angela said miserably. "I don't know anything any more. I don't know who to talk to or trust."

"You can talk to me. You can trust me," Theo said.

Angela regarded him, then turned away.

Tell me what's going on. *Tell me*. Theo willed Angela to talk to him. He didn't want to push her. He sensed that she would clam up altogether if he did that.

"M-My brother Tom and three of his friends are going to do a job on Wednesday." Angela's voice was so low Theo had to strain to hear it.

"A job?"

"They're up to something ... dodgy. I don't know what. They were still planning it last week. Tom doesn't like to leave me alone when he's not at home unless he doesn't have any choice so he ... he took me to his meetings..."

"Meetings?" Theo prompted.

"The meetings where Tom, Scott, Robbie and Dylan made all their plans. I had to stay in the office on the first floor. It's glass fronted so they could see me from the ground floor but with the door shut I couldn't hear what they were saying. That's why I wanted you to go into the ventilator shaft and listen to them for me. I thought you could be my ears."

"And Ricky went instead of me..."

"And got caught," Angela said. "He's exactly the last person I would've asked to do something like this. He's not exactly quiet, is he? They probably heard him making a noise within the first five seconds that he arrived."

"Don't you dare make it sound like it's Ricky's fault," Theo exploded. "If anything happens to him, I'll never forgive myself – or *you*."

"I didn't want him to get caught. I didn't want anyone to get into trouble. I just needed to know what was going on, what Tom was getting himself into," Angela insisted.

Theo bit back the harsh words ready to explode from his mouth. He counted to ten quickly, then added another fifteen for good measure.

"So how much do you know about what your brother and his friends are up to?" he asked at last.

"Not much. I know that whatever it is, it's going to happen on Wednesday. Wednesday night," Angela said. "Tom said that Ricky would be released on Thursday morning if everything went according to plan."

"Thursday? What about Ricky's mum?

She's going through hell and you're going to make her wait until Thursday before letting her know that Ricky's all right?" Theo couldn't believe it.

"I've got no choice. Robbie and Scott already think I'm involved. Theo, you don't know them. If the police or anyone else for that matter tries to move in on them, Ricky will get hurt – or worse."

"Your brother's got some really charming friends!" Theo wasn't impressed.

"Don't you judge him." Angela rounded on Theo like a rabid dog. "Tom's had to look after me all by himself since I was seven. He even stood up to our social workers when they wanted to put me in a foster home. So don't you say a thing against him."

"I'm not going to argue with you," Theo replied frostily. "All I want to do is rescue Ricky."

"Rescue? I thought you just wanted to make sure he was safe…"

"I want to get him away from your brother and his friends."

Silence.

"Are you going to help me do that or not?" Theo urged.

"I'll … I'll try."

"Not good enough," said Theo immediately. "Either you're with me on this or you're not. And if you're not, I'll go to the police."

"That's blackmail," Angela protested.

"Angela, wake up! Your brother and his friends aren't up to something dodgy or cagey or shady or any other stupid word like that. They've kidnapped Ricky. And God knows what they're going to do on Wednesday night. But whatever it is, it's obviously illegal. Not dodgy, cagey or shady. *Illegal!* When are you going to open your eyes and see that?"

"I'm not listening." Angela put her hands over her ears.

Theo tried to pull Angela's arms down by her sides. She battled to keep her hands where they were.

"All right! All right! We'll play it your way. There's nothing *illegal* going on at all! Your brother and his friends are angels!" Theo said with biting sarcasm. "So what's the next step?"

Slowly, Angela's arms dropped back down to her sides.

"I'll talk to Tom when I get home, then I'll meet you afterwards and tell you what I know," she sniffed.

"When?"

"Eight o'clock?"

"Fine. Where?"

"The park. The swings in the playground."

"I'll be there," Theo said.

Angela walked away down the corridor. Theo watched her go for a few moments before calling out to her.

"Angela?"

Angela turned her head.

"If you don't turn up…" Theo left the rest unsaid.

Angela's eyes blazed at him with a hatred that would have knocked Theo backwards if he hadn't already been up against the wall. Without a word she turned her head and carried on walking. Theo's frown deepened as he watched her turn the corner. He didn't like blackmailing her, it left a nasty taste in his mouth and a horrible churning feeling in his stomach, but what else could he do? There was no way Angela was going to help him unless he cajoled and bullied and coaxed her every step of the way.

So what would she do? Suppose she didn't turn up? Theo sighed. In a way that would make things a lot easier. Theo could then just go to the police and let them find Ricky. If Angela *did* turn up, then Theo would be letting himself in for goodness only knew what.

But, hang on – suppose Angela didn't turn up but sent someone else instead? What if she told her brother or his friends what Theo was trying to do? They'd be waiting for him in the park and then he might end up in exactly the same place and predicament as Ricky. A fat lot of good he'd be to his friend then. Theo didn't trust Angela, not by a long way. She could easily tell her brother about him and then what?

"So what're you going to do?" Theo asked himself.

But he already knew the answer. He was going to take a chance and turn up at the park at eight o'clock. And he was going to be very, *very* careful.

11 THEO KNOWS

17:30hrs Monday, 19th May

Theo knows…
I have no choice now. I've got to tell Tom about Theo. I have to. Tom's my brother and I can't let Theo spoil things for us. Since I wrote in here this morning, things have got worse, not better. When is it all going to end? *Where* is it going to end? I have to stop writing now.

I'm smudging the ink across the paper again.

12 BETRAYED

Theo crouched down before taking a look around. The warning bells in his head wouldn't stop clanging.

Go to the police… Go to the police…

On and on they rang. Theo shook his head. Try as he might, he couldn't get over the feeling that he was being really, *really* stupid. Here he was in the park at twenty-five minutes past eight – and all alone… How much longer should he wait? It looked like Angela wasn't coming. Maybe she never had any intention of turning up. Maybe she'd just sent her brother and his friends… And what if Tom and the others *did* turn up? Theo wouldn't know any of them from Adam. He could easily end up in the same predicament as Ricky before he had time to blink.

Theo checked his position again. He should be safe where he was. He was crouched down behind an oak tree on a slope leading down to the fenced-off stream. At the first sign of anything suspicious he'd leg it down the slope, hop over the fence and he'd race down the shallow stream towards the woods. He'd move so fast, Tom and his friends wouldn't see him for the water spray!

Theo frowned down at his watch. He'd give her until twenty-five to nine. After that… Hang on! That man over there… Could he be Angela's brother? They looked quite similar. Theo crouched even lower.

"Come on, Angela," he muttered.

Where was she?

As if the thought summoned the person, Angela turned into the park and started walking down the path towards the children's playground. Theo froze. He didn't dare risk showing himself. Not until he knew she had come alone. He looked around again to see if anyone was watching her or acting suspiciously. There were plenty of people in the park, children and adults. It was hard to tell who was with whom.

Angela was getting closer... Soon she would draw level with his hidden position behind the tree. Theo stood up slowly, careful to still keep himself hidden. A tall, slim man with dark hair and wearing a T-shirt and faded jeans turned into the park and immediately raced towards Angela. The man called out to her and she spun around. The moment she saw him, they launched into a fierce argument. Theo was too far away to hear all they were saying but they were obviously both very angry. Theo moved further into the shadow of the tree.

"Gotcha!" A vice-like hand descended on Theo's shoulder, the fingers digging into his flesh like talons.

Theo jumped out of his skin. He turned and the world was filled with the bearded face of a stranger. A stranger whose eyes burned into Theo with angry satisfaction. Theo's whole body felt like it was being held together with paperclips. Only the stranger's hand on his shoulder kept him upright and on his feet. He'd been set up. Angela had betrayed him…

"What d'you think you're doing – skulking about, hiding behind trees? I've been watching you. I want to know what you're up to."

Theo hardly heard a word. The only sound in the world was that of his heart racing at light speed. The only sight was the stranger's angry glare. Theo felt the stranger's moist breath whisper over his face. It smelt of fresh coffee and stale cigarettes. Theo opened and closed his mouth like a fish out of water. The stranger drew back slightly and frowned.

"Are you all right?" he asked.

Slowly the world stopped crazily rocking. Theo blinked, then blinked again.

The stranger's words replayed in his mind. Theo took in more of the stranger's appearance now. He was the Park-keeper! It wasn't just his uniform that gave it away – the badge on his lapel which said PARK-KEEPER was another big clue!

"What's the matter? Are you ill?" asked the Park-keeper.

Theo nodded. It wasn't a lie. The churning in his stomach was only just beginning to slow down.

"What're you doing?" asked the Park-keeper.

"Waiting for someone," breathed Theo. He shrugged out of the Park-keeper's grasp.

"What were you going to do? Leap out at them?"

Theo didn't answer. The Park-keeper took a step back.

"Look, are you OK? I didn't mean to scare you. I thought you were one of those yobbo boys who's been jumping out at people from behind trees – upsetting people, scaring them half to death," the Park-keeper sniffed indignantly.

"Well, I wasn't doing that," said Theo. "You're the one who frightened *me*."

"Hhmm! Well, I'll let you off – this once," said the Park-keeper.

"You can't let me off if I wasn't doing anything in the first place," Theo pointed out.

The Park-keeper was in the wrong but he couldn't bring himself to apologize to a kid. He was a typical grown-up, Theo fumed.

"Just watch yourself," said the Park-keeper.

And off he marched. Theo glared after him. Then he remembered. Angela! Theo turned around. Angela and the man she'd been arguing with had gone…

13 THE NO-SHOW

Theo pushed against the front door. It closed with a click that had him holding his breath. It was past nine. He was meant to be home by eight-thirty at the very latest. So much for all his plans. So much for finding out where Ricky was being held and devising a plan to rescue him. Theo's head was spinning. He just wanted to lie down for a while, clear his head and think about what he should do next. Anxiously, he looked towards the living-room. Nothing. Theo tiptoed to the stairs, then stopped. What should he do now? Tiptoe or charge? The stairs creaked horribly. If he tiptoed he was bound to get caught. But he'd get caught for sure if he charged. Theo sighed. He was going to get caught, no matter how he went up the stairs, so he might as well get it over with. Theo started walking upstairs normally. Charging required too much energy and tiptoeing required too much effort. He'd barely got his foot on the third stair when his mum and dad flew out of the living-room.

"Where on earth have you been?" Dad raged.

"I went to the park," Theo said.

"Until almost ten o'clock? We were worried sick."

Theo glanced down at his watch. It was twenty minutes past nine, not "almost ten", but Theo prudently decided not to argue.

"Sorry…" he began.

"Sorry! Sorry! Is that all you have to say?" Mum asked.

"I didn't realize it was so late." Theo tried to explain.

He got no further. A policeman with wispy brown hair and a short, neat beard came out of the living-room. Theo stared. What had happened? Why was the policeman here?

"As I was saying, Mr and Mrs Mosley, when children disappear, nine times out of ten there's a perfectly reasonable, logical explanation!" said the policeman.

"I'm sorry. We seem to have wasted your time," Dad said grittily.

"No trouble. I'm just glad Theo turned up safe and sound," said the policeman.

Theo's breath caught in his throat. The policeman was there because of *him*.

Dad escorted the policeman to the front door.

"I'll radio it in that your son has been found," the policeman said.

"Yes. Thank you," said Dad. "I'm sorry you were called out unnecessarily."

"That's OK. Good night." The policeman opened the door and cast Theo a sympathetic glance before shutting the door behind him. Theo looked at his mum and dad. They glared back at him. It was like standing at the edge of an erupting volcano. Theo's whole body was burning up.

"Where's your watch?" Dad asked, his dark eyes glinting like chips of granite.

Reluctantly, Theo held out his left wrist.

"You had your watch on and you didn't know what time it was?" said Dad.

"I … I didn't look at it," Theo replied.

"Theo, how could you be so thoughtless?" Mum asked. "Ricky's disappeared and you've seen what his mum is going through. How could you put us through the same thing?"

Mum's voice was quiet and sad. Somehow that was worse than her yelling at him.

"What were you doing in the park?" Dad asked.

"I … I was just thinking. I was trying to help Ricky." And that was the truth, even if it wasn't the *whole* truth.

"Trying to help Ricky – how?" said Dad.

Theo struggled to find the right words. What was he supposed to say? I went to meet a girl in my class called Angela, because her brother is holding Ricky against his will, only she disappeared before I had the chance to speak to her. Maybe that's exactly what he *should* say. Get it all out into the open. He had to think of Ricky.

Just as Theo opened his mouth, the phone rang. Still frowning at Theo, Dad walked across the hall to answer it.

"Hello?"

Dad's frown deepened as he listened. Theo took a step down the stairs. Was it something about Ricky?

"I'm afraid he's busy at the moment... It is rather late to be phoning my son..." Dad said tersely.

Theo stepped forward again. He instinctively knew who was at the other end of the phone.

"It's someone called Angela. This is the third time she's called in five minutes. She says it's important," Dad said.

Theo stepped forward, reaching out for the receiver.

"We want to see you when you've finished," Dad said, before handing it over.

Theo waited until his mum and dad went back into the living-room before lifting the receiver to his ear.

"What happened?" Theo hissed.

"I tried to sneak out but Tom came after me." Angela's voice was so low that Theo had to strain to hear it. "He insisted on taking me home."

Theo checked. His mum and dad weren't listening. Even so, he turned his back to the living-room and lowered his voice.

"What about Ricky? D'you know where he is?"

There was a noticeable pause before Angela answered.

"No. I don't know where he is now, but I do know where he'll be tomorrow night. With your help, we can get him away from Robbie."

Theo took a quick glance around to make sure that he was still alone.

"Why should I believe you? Why don't I just tell Mum and Dad what I already know about you and your brother and Robbie and all the others?"

"Because you don't have any proof," Angela replied immediately. "Because it'd be my word against yours. And the moment another

111

grown-up gets involved, you'd never see Ricky alive again – Robbie will make sure of that. Is that what you want?"

Theo clenched his free hand, totally frustrated that he could do nothing else.

"A-Are you still there?" The quiver in Angela's voice revealed that she wasn't quite as in control as Theo had first thought.

"Yes, I'm still here," Theo replied. "So where will Ricky be tomorrow night?"

"I'll tell you when I see you," Angela said at last.

Theo understood at once. What he didn't know, he couldn't tell anyone else.

"But you'll really help me get Ricky away from your brother's friends?" Theo asked.

"I said so, didn't I?" Angela snapped.

"Then I'll see you at school tomorrow morning," said Theo.

"After school," Angela contradicted.

"What d'you mean…? Hello?"

The continuous purr of the telephone line was the only answer. Angela had hung up on him.

"Theo?"

Theo spun around at the sound of his mum's voice. Had she heard…? No, her expression was still the same as before the phone call. He followed her into the living-room.

"I'm sorry I was late home, Mum and Dad," Theo said quickly. "I didn't mean to worry you."

"Well, you did," said Dad, still not placated.

"I know. I won't do it again," Theo said. "I promise."

"Hhmm! I want you home straight after school every night this week. Is that clear?" said Mum.

But Theo was meant to meet Angela after school the next day…

"Theo, answer your mother," Dad ordered.

"It's clear," Theo mumbled, his fingers discreetly crossed at his sides.

"D'you want something to eat?" Mum asked reluctantly. She was still angry with him but she was always, always worried that he hadn't eaten enough – no matter what time of the day or night!

Theo shook his head.

"…the hunt for Richard Burridge. This report from Julia Bartless."

Instantly all eyes turned towards the TV screen. The image switched from the newscaster to a black woman reporter. Theo's mouth dropped open. He pointed at the block of flats behind the reporter.

"That's…"

"I'm standing outside the flats where Ricky Burridge lives with his mother," the reporter began. "Ricky, aged eleven, disappeared three days ago."

Ricky's photograph filled the screen.

"Police are very concerned about Ricky and are mounting a house-to-house investigation in the area, but they admit that hope and time are running out," the reporter concluded.

The newscaster in the news studio appeared again on the left-hand side of the TV with the reporter on a screen above him and to the right. The newscaster turned to the reporter and asked, "Have you had a chance to speak to Ricky's mother yet?"

Julia Bartless shook her head. "Mrs Burridge was too upset to speak to us and is currently being comforted by friends and relatives."

"Do the police have any clues at all?" asked the newscaster.

"Not as yet, but as one policewoman told me, they're going to intensify their search until Ricky is found."

Theo's stomach churned. His blood roared throughout his body. It was horrible – worse than horrible. Ricky's mum had to be going through hell. Theo remembered what she'd looked like on Friday morning and now more days had gone past. Theo's mum came over to him and put an arm around his shoulders.

"Your dad and I can't watch you every single second of the day so we just have to trust you to be careful and sensible," she said.

Theo nodded, searching desperately for something to say.

"Ricky will turn up all right, I know he will," he said at last.

Mum smiled faintly.

"Let's hope so, Theo," Dad sighed. "Let's hope so."

And in that moment, Theo's mind was made up. He *was* going to meet Angela after school tomorrow and deal with the consequences afterwards.

But later, as Theo cleaned his teeth, he couldn't get a phrase out of his head. It kept repeating like a song he couldn't get out of his mind.

Fools rush in…

14 THE ESCAPE

22:55 hrs Monday, 19th May

I hate him. HATE, HATE, HATE him!

When I got home from school today, they were all in our house. I'd barely got my key out of the front door when Robbie said he was going to lock me in my room. And Tom let him. Tom looked down at the ground, at the walls, at his shoes – anywhere but at me. Scott and Dylan didn't say a word either. No one stuck up for me. There was no one on my side. Tom asked Robbie if locking me in my room was "really necessary".

Really necessary! I think it's just as well I

didn't tell Tom about Theo and what happened at school today. He'd have run straight to Robbie. It's as if he's afraid to think for himself unless Robbie tells him when and how.

I told Robbie I was meant to be meeting someone in the park. D'you know what he said?

"Tough! You'll stay in and do as you're told."

And then he had the extra nerve to tell me that I couldn't go to school tomorrow.

"We've got something lined up for tomorrow evening and we can't risk anything or anyone lousing it up for us," he told me.

"How does my going to school louse things up for you?" I asked.

"You're not going to school tomorrow and that's final," Robbie replied.

And all the time, Tom said nothing. I was so furious I threw a tantrum on the bed and beat up my pillow. How could Tom let Robbie do that to me? How *could* he?

I racked my brains all evening to think of

some way of getting out of my room without any of them downstairs finding out. I finally had to sneak out of my bedroom window, across the flat roof and down the drainpipe. I was positive that at any moment, I'd feel Robbie's fingers digging into my arms.

I HATE HIM!

I scraped practically all the skin off my knees and there's hardly any left on the palms of my hands either. But I got out. Only, Tom caught up with me in the park before I'd a chance to talk to Theo. Tom was furious. And he said that Scott and especially Robbie were spitting nails! I just hope Theo didn't see us. Theo doesn't trust me as it is. Goodness only knows what he would've thought if he saw Tom with me. I had to beg Tom to at least let me phone my friend to let him know why I didn't show up. I refused to budge until he agreed.

When we got home, you should've heard Robbie's language. I'm surprised the air around his head didn't turn bright blue. Tom hustled me straight to my bedroom, even though Robbie wanted to question me. For once Tom stood up for me. That happens so rarely – no wonder I'm writing it in my diary.

Tom sneaked me the telephone directory and let me use his mobile phone. I got through half the Mosleys in the book before I reached Theo's house. I think I got to him just in time. I hope I managed to convince him not to do anything stupid.

When the other sharks had left, Tom tried to tell me not to worry. I asked him what was going on.

"Nothing that concerns you. But after tomorrow we'll be on easy street. We'll have money enough to last us the rest of our lives. I'll be able to look after you properly, without social workers sticking their noses into our business every five seconds."

My heart sank at that.

"Tom, I don't know what you're up to, but whatever it is that Robbie wants you to do, don't do it. You're going to get into trouble. I can feel it."

"Don't talk wet," Tom laughed.

"What about Ricky?" I asked. I could feel the tears pricking at my eyes then.

"I don't want to talk about … about the boy," Tom said icily. "After tomorrow he'll be fine."

"But how d'you know that? How d'you know…?"

"I don't want to hear it," Tom interrupted. He had that funny, glassy look in his eyes and I knew he'd stopped listening to me. He always does that when someone says something that he doesn't want to hear. So I just gave up after that. There's no point in talking to Tom when he switches off. He tried to change the subject and make me laugh the way he always does when I'm feeling sad but I didn't laugh and I didn't say a word. He soon took the hint. I'm still mad at him. He's like a sheep when it comes to Robbie. It's like his brain just melts away every time Robbie gets within a kilometre of him.

But I'm not going to let Robbie have things all his own way. This business with Ricky has gone far enough.

15 WATCHING THE WAREHOUSE

Theo looked up and down the street. *Where was she?*

Right! That's it, Theo thought angrily. He'd had more than enough of all this messing about. He was going straight round the nearest...

"Theo? Theo!"

Theo turned his head. Angela came running down the street at full pelt towards him. He took a quick look around. No grown-ups were lurking – at least none that he could see. It looked like Angela was alone.

"I wasn't sure if you'd turn up," Theo admitted once Angela caught up to him.

"To be honest, I wasn't sure either," Angela confessed.

They both looked at each other and tentatively smiled. Then Theo remembered Ricky and his smile faded to nothing.

"We'll have to be very careful," Angela said. "Robbie's brought the job forward to tonight."

"Tonight! How d'you know?"

"Tom's had me packing our suitcases all day. We're supposed to be going on holiday tonight…"

"On holiday? Where?"

"Tom didn't tell me. He said it was a surprise," Angela replied grimly.

"And what *is* this job they're doing tonight?"

"I don't know."

"But we can rescue Ricky – right?"

Angela nodded, crossing her fingers behind her back where Theo couldn't see.

"Then let's get going," said Theo.

Angela turned around and started walking back the way she'd just come.

"Where're we going?" Theo asked, falling into step next to her.

Angela looked at Theo steadily. "To the warehouse on Buzan Road."

"But … but the police have already searched that place," Theo frowned.

"Which is why they've moved back there. The police have searched it once so they won't search it again. Scott reckoned it'd be safe for tonight."

"How d'you know all this?" Theo asked suspiciously.

"I heard some of what they were saying in the kitchen when I climbed out of my bedroom window last night," Angela explained. And that wasn't all she'd heard. Most of Scott's conversation had been about Ricky – and it was terrifying…

"You climbed out of your window? Why did you do that?"

"It was the only way I could meet you in the park. Robbie locked me in my bedroom," Angela explained.

Theo gasped and stared at Angela. "Robbie sounds like a real prince and two-thirds."

"He's that all right," Angela said bitterly.

"What happened when you got back home? Are you OK?" Theo asked, concerned.

Angela shrugged. "Yeah, I'll survive. Thanks for asking."

Theo's face began to burn. His face set hard and he glared at Angela.

"I was only being nosy, that's all. It doesn't mean we're engaged or anything."

"I never said it did." Angela's smile broadened.

Other thoughts bubbling up in Theo's mind refused to stay buried.

"Now d'you see why I want to get Ricky away from Robbie and the others? What makes you think that Robbie's going to keep his word and release Ricky?" The words erupted from Theo like a volcanic explosion.

"Tom wouldn't let anyone hurt Ricky…"

"Tom couldn't stop Robbie from locking you in your room. What makes you think he could stand up to Robbie and Scott and the other one?" Theo said. "What makes you think he'd even want to?"

"Shut up! SHUT UP!" Angela screamed at him.

They glared at each other like two enemies

having a show-down in one of the old Western films. Theo carried on walking first. Angela fell into step with him. They walked in silence to the end of the road.

"Wait a sec," said Theo, as they neared the phone box at the corner of the street.

Stepping into the kiosk, Theo picked up the receiver and began to dial, pressing more and more firmly on each numbered key.

"Who're you phoning?" Angela asked warily.

"My mum and dad. Neither of them will be home from work yet – at least I hope not."

"I don't understand."

"I'm going… Hang on!" Theo listened intently to what was going on at the other end of the phone. "Hi Mum, Dad. A girl in my class, Angela Tukesbury, asked me to help her with her homework. I'm going round to her house now. I hope that's all right."

Angela realized what was going on. Theo was talking into an answering machine.

"It shouldn't take too long. Angela said I could have dinner at her house and then her mum or dad will give me a lift home," Theo continued at a rush. "See you soon. 'Bye."

Theo put the phone down quickly as if he was afraid that the receiver itself might start arguing with him.

"You shouldn't have said that about my mum and dad," said Angela.

"Why not?"

"I live with my brother, Tom. There isn't anyone else. I told you that before."

"What happened to your parents?" Theo asked curiously.

"Mum ran off when I was five and Dad died a couple of years later."

"How old was your brother then?" said Theo.

"Old enough to take care of me," Angela rounded on him.

"OK! OK! Don't bite my head off. I only asked," Theo said quickly.

"Sorry," Angela mumbled. "But ever since Dad died that's all I've heard. Tom's not old enough, Tom's not responsible enough. Everyone's so desperate to get me into a children's home."

"Tom's not going to do you much good if he and his friends are caught on this job they're doing and sent to prison," Theo pointed out.

"It won't come to that. And don't be such a smart alec doof ball," Angela fumed.

Theo opened his mouth to argue, only to snap it shut without saying a word. The last thing he wanted was to antagonize Angela, and besides, it *had* been the sort of thing a doof would say!

Theo and Angela lapsed into silence until they reached Buzan Road. Each step that took them closer to the warehouse had Theo's heart pounding just that bit harder. About ten metres away from the warehouse, Angela's hand on Theo's arm stopped him in his tracks. They both stood in silence.

"What happens now?" Theo asked, still looking at the warehouse.

"We have to get into the ventilation shaft and wait. When they leave tonight to do their job, that's when we rescue Ricky."

"They're all inside the warehouse now –

right? Tom, Robbie, Scott and…?"

"Dylan."

"And Ricky?"

"And Ricky."

"And whatever it is they're up to, it's definitely going to happen tonight?" Theo asked.

Angela nodded. "That's why Tom left me at home instead of taking me with him as usual. He said he wanted me to get a good night's sleep for once – as if I'd believe that! He's dragged me to the warehouse with him every night for the last two weeks whilst they've been planning whatever it is they're up to."

"Why didn't he just leave you at home?"

"Tom worries about me," Angela shrugged. "The house might catch fire, it might get hit by lightning, crushed by an alien ship landing on it – anything."

Theo raised his eyebrows.

"That's how Tom thinks," Angela smiled ruefully. "He reckoned I was safer with him. Except for tonight when they're going to do whatever it is they've been planning for so long. I haven't got to sleep before three in the morning in over a fortnight."

"So that's why you're always yawning in class," Theo realized.

"No, I'm not," Angela frowned.

"Yes, you are."

"I don't yawn in class," Angela said belligerently.

"If you say so." Theo shrugged as he regarded her.

What was it with Angela anyway? If there was anything she didn't like or didn't agree with, she'd say it didn't happen, or deny it or just blank it out. Like drawing the curtains on reality and saying that the world beyond her window didn't exist.

"What're you looking at?" Angela scowled.

"From where I'm standing – not much!" Theo snapped back.

They both turned to look back at the warehouse, each of them burning with a different kind of anger inside.

"How d'you know they're not going to take Ricky with them tonight?" asked Theo.

"I heard Tom trying to persuade the rest to leave Ricky behind. He said Ricky would only be in the way."

"Did he succeed?"

"I hope so. We'll soon find out," Angela replied. "Scott … Scott mentioned something about taking Ricky with them to use as a hostage in case anything went wrong."

Theo stared at her. Fear like a giant wave crashed over him, leaving him breathless.

"But maybe Tom managed to change his mind," Angela continued desperately.

Silence. Theo took a deep breath.

"Come on. Let's get Ricky out of there," Theo said at last.

Cautiously, they both approached the warehouse. Theo looked up and down the street. No one *seemed* to be watching them.

"Are you sure they haven't posted a lookout?" Theo whispered.

Angela looked up and down the street as well. "I don't see anyone."

They peered down the side alleyway where the ventilator shaft was situated. Two cars

131

were there now which hadn't been there before. One was a metallic grey Escort. The other was dark blue, but Theo couldn't see what make of car it was. After a brief look at each other, Angela and Theo tiptoed down the alley.

"Oh, no! Look!" Theo pointed when they were a couple of metres away from the grille.

Angela saw at once what the problem was. The metallic grey Escort was parked too close to the grille. It would be a real battle to try and get the grille off, let alone squeeze into the tiny space left between the car and the ventilator shaft.

"What do we do now?" Angela whispered.

Theo's eyes narrowed with determination. "We don't give up. Not now we're so close."

Reluctantly, Angela nodded.

"Come on, Angela." Theo beckoned, moving forward.

They both eased their way between the Escort and the wall. Leaning back against the car's front wheel arch, Theo interlaced his fingers into the grille. He could get his fingers into the mesh all right, but he was so close to it, he couldn't get enough force behind his attempts to pull.

"Help then!" Theo urged.

Angela tried, but it was no use. The grille didn't budge.

"We're going to have to think of something else," Angela sighed.

On the main road, someone coughed, then sneezed violently.

"Why don't you get something for that?" a man's voice asked irritably. "You've been coughing all over us for the last two days."

Angela's eyes widened with horror.

"Move! Quick!" she hissed.

"What's the ma…?"

"MOVE!" she ordered urgently, pushing Theo away from her.

Theo fell on to his hands and crawled away as fast as he could.

"What's going…?"

"Quick! Please…" Angela implored.

Theo ducked behind the Escort, immediately followed by Angela. They both squatted down as low as possible between the two cars, just as footsteps turned into the alleyway.

"I don't like it, Dylan. What's Robbie up to in there?" A man's voice accompanied the sets of footsteps that turned into the alleyway.

"I don't know and I ain't gonna ask," came the reply.

"Who…?" Theo began.

Angela shook her head quickly, her finger over her lips. She turned and pointed to the second car behind them. Theo nodded. He peeped his head out from his side of the car. It seemed all clear. The two men must be walking on the other side of the alleyway. He could see the swinging arm and shoulder of one of the men and the side of his face but that was it. To be honest, Theo didn't want to see any more than that. He beckoned with his head and started crawling alongside the second car. The men were still talking and getting closer and closer. Theo was so busy concentrating on the men behind him that he didn't see the sharp piece of rubble beneath him – but his knee felt it. He only just managed to bite his lip in time to stop himself from crying out. Theo raised his knee slightly, brushing the debris off his jeans. He wasn't surprised when his hand came away smeared with red. His knee was bleeding. Grimacing at the pain, Theo carried on moving until he reached the back of the second car with Angela only moments behind him. They both sat back against the car, making themselves as low as possible.

"What's Robbie going to do with the boy?" the first man asked.

"Dunno," Dylan replied, brusquely.

"I hope he's not stupid enough to bring him along," said the first man.

"Look at it from Robbie's point of view. That boy knows all our plans, everything we're up to – and he's seen our faces…" Dylan's words trailed away into silence.

"But he can't hurt us after tonight. Besides, who'd take the word of a boy over four grown-ups?" the first voice argued.

"I don't like it any better than you," said Dylan. And from the sound of his voice, he really didn't. "But are you going to argue with Robbie? 'Cause I sure as hell ain't." Then the same man had a coughing fit.

Theo didn't realize he was holding his breath until his chest started to hurt. And still he didn't dare to breathe. The pain in his knee was sharp and intense, his lungs were aching fit to burst and he didn't dare twitch an eyelid.

"Let it go," Dylan continued. "Unless you've got a death wish."

"But that boy…"

"That boy is none of our concern. And we'd better not still be here when Robbie comes out or we'll be in trouble ourselves," Dylan interrupted.

Theo heard a clunk, then the sound of car doors opening.

"I still don't like it – not one little…" The rest of what the first man was saying was cut off by the car door slamming. Moments later the engine started. Only then did Theo release his breath in an audible hiss, dragging air into his tortured lungs with the next gasp.

"We've got to move – fast." Theo whispered as he turned to Angela.

Angela stared straight ahead, tears overflowing from her eyes and running down her cheeks to drip on to her lap.

"Angela…?"

"That was Dylan who got into the car," Angela whispered. "Dylan and my brother, Tom…"

16 GOTCHA!

"Angela? Angela, listen to me," Theo pleaded. "Your brother's all right. He's safe, but you heard what they said. Ricky isn't. D'you hear me?"

"Tom said he wasn't really involved, he said he was just helping with the planning ... but he's up to his neck in all this," Angela sobbed.

"Your brother's not up to his neck. He passed that when they kidnapped Ricky. He's way, *way* over his head," Theo argued. "Angela, you've got to help me. We don't have much time."

"He lied to me. Tom lied to me..."

Theo squatted down in front of Angela, taking her by the arms and shaking her.

"Angela, help me – *please*."

Angela looked straight through him.

"Right then. I'll do it myself. You sit there!" Theo said, angrily.

He leapt up and ran over to the grille. The Escort had gone so now he could use all his strength to pull it off – and he needed to get the grille off in a hurry. From what Dylan and Tom had said, Robbie would be out next and he was the very last person Theo wanted to meet. He *had* to get to Ricky. Theo interlaced his fingers in the grille and pulled as hard as he could. Nothing happened. He tugged harder, leaning back so that his whole weight could be used to pull the grille off. The metal bit into his fingers even worse than before but Theo couldn't give up. Not now. Angela laced her fingers into the grille and pulled alongside Theo. Theo looked at her, then got back to the task in hand.

"Really pull – after three," Theo panted. "One…"

"Two…"

"Three!"

There came a faint grating sound and then the grille flew off its mounting. Angela and Theo ended up sprawled on the ground, still clutching the grille.

"Let's get going," Theo said, disentangling himself.

He took a deep breath, then another, before crawling into the shaft. He wasn't looking forward to being in that musty, dusty, cramped space again, but now not just minutes but seconds counted.

"Theo, help!"

Theo turned his head to see Angela struggling with the grille. Making himself as small as possible, Theo turned around. He and Angela struggled to pull the grille back on. Theo's fingers were already red raw from pulling at the grille but he couldn't risk Robbie or anyone else coming out of the warehouse and noticing something was wrong. With one last effort, he and Angela heaved the grille back in place.

"Will it stay put?" Angela asked, doubt-fully.

"Let's hope so," Theo said. "Come on."

They crawled together side by side until the tunnel became too narrow, then Theo led the way. The dust danced around them, the light grew dimmer and the smell was even worse than before – something Theo wouldn't have thought possible. When he reached the section of the tunnel which branched off to the right and left as well as straight ahead, he stopped.

"We need to get to the basement," Angela whispered from behind him.

Theo looked up and down the tunnels, his eyes narrowed with concentration.

"This way," he said at last, turning to his right.

"How d'you know that?" Angela asked, surprised.

"I've been in here before," Theo replied.

"You have?"

"Yeah, on Monday morning."

"So that's why you were late," Angela breathed. "I wondered."

"Shush!" Theo whispered nervously.

The end of the tunnel was in sight. Cautiously, they moved towards it. Once there, Theo looked through the mesh down towards the basement. Three or four low-wattage light bulbs provided the only light. Though it was bright outside, Theo's eyes took a few moments to adjust to the gloom in the basement.

A white man with light brown hair tied back in a pony-tail stood below, his back towards the ventilator shaft. A smallish table, a large mattress and a couple of rickety, wooden chairs were the only bits of furniture that Theo could see – furniture that hadn't been there before. He turned his head this way and that, searching for Ricky.

"What's going on? Budge over," Angela whispered.

"Shush!" Theo urged.

There was barely room for him, let alone enough for Angela to see what was going on as well.

"Budge up," Angela insisted.

Angela pushed Theo's legs out of her way. Theo had to lie on his side to allow Angela to crawl forward. They both watched through the mesh as the man with the pony-tail packed a dark holdall with assorted items off the table. He picked up something and Theo caught a quick glimpse of it before the man put it in his jacket pocket. A gun...

"There's two men down there..." Theo whispered.

"That's Robbie." Angela nodded towards the man with the pony-tail. "And that's Scott, Robbie's brother." She pointed to the other man. Scott's hair did little more than patchily cover his head, it was so short. He was tall and broad and wore army combat clothes and what looked like Doc Martens. Theo didn't like the look of him at all. He was definitely *not* the sort of guy you wanted to meet on a dark night – nor even in broad daylight come to that. Neither of them were. Robbie picked up the holdall.

"All set?" Scott asked his brother.

Robbie nodded, then said something about

"the boy" which Theo didn't catch. Theo inched closer.

"What about Dylan and Tom?" Scott asked.

"What about them?" Robbie replied.

The two brothers regarded each other, before they both burst out laughing. Theo's blood ran ice-cold in his veins at the sound. He glanced at Angela. The grim look on her face reflected what Theo was thinking. Robbie and Scott were up to something ... evil. Something that even Dylan and Tom didn't know about.

"Take care of business, Scott. And don't be late to the Irving. I need you. I'll take care of the boy." And with that, Robbie headed for the exit at the far end of the basement. Theo and Angela watched him leave before either of them spoke.

"What did Robbie mean by that – 'I'll take care of the boy'?" Theo asked.

Angela didn't answer.

"I don't see Ricky," said Theo.

"He should be here." Angela looked

around. "Maybe they've got him tied up on the ground floor somewhere. I'll go and take a look."

"No, don't. We should stick together..." But Theo was wasting his breath. Already Angela was wriggling backwards.

"Angela!" Theo called after her.

It was no use. Theo shook his head. Angela was going to get them into real trouble at this rate. With a start, Theo realized what he'd just done.

He'd called after Angela *out loud*...

Theo ducked his head immediately. Had Scott heard him? Theo's stomach churned. He could taste fear, bitter as bile, in his mouth. Don't start panicking, he told himself sternly. Scott probably hadn't heard a thing. Theo raised his head slowly and looked down through the dust-covered mesh.

"I see you..." Scott said softly.

Scott stood directly underneath the grille, staring straight up at him. Theo's breath caught in his throat. His blood froze. In that instant, his whole body went numb.

Slowly, Scott raised his hand and pointed at Theo. "Stay there!" he ordered.

Theo didn't wait to hear anything else. Panic-stricken, he pushed himself backwards. Stay? Yeah, likely! He had to get out of there – *fast*. In the shaft, he was a sitting duck. Ahead, Theo heard footsteps hurrying, then the sound of something being dragged across the concrete floor.

He's after me, Theo thought desperately.

Digging his elbows and knees into the floor, Theo used them to propel himself backwards. Ignoring the pain that the hard flooring and the bits of debris and rubble caused him as they bit into his skin, Theo could think of nothing else but getting out of there. How he wished he could turn around. Scott wouldn't be able to see him for the dust – literally! – if he could just turn around.

"Where d'you think you're going?" Scott's face appeared at the shaft.

He's standing on the table, Theo realized. Within moments, Scott wrenched off the grille and threw it behind him. It crashed to the floor, the sound echoing throughout the warehouse and straight through Theo's head. Now there was nothing between him and Scott.

"Gotcha!" Scott lunged at Theo, just missing him.

With a sob of pure fear, Theo scurried back faster, using every part of his body, wriggling like a snake.

Scott placed both hands in the shaft and heaved himself upwards, trying to get after Theo. Only he cracked his head on the top of the shaft and sank out of sight, swearing fluently.

"I hope you've cracked your head wide open!" Theo called after him, still scurrying backwards.

Ahead, he heard the sound of running footsteps, but strangely enough they were running away from him rather than towards him. Puzzled, Theo slowed down, then stopped. Where was Scott going? Why wasn't he coming after him? Theo got up on all fours, wondering why he hadn't done it sooner. It would've been so much easier to move. He leaned forward and listened very carefully. Silence. What was Scott up to? The silence stretched on for ever.

Then Theo realized. Scott was going to come up behind him. That was the only explanation. He hurled himself forward, not stopping until he got to the grille opening. The basement seemed all clear, but maybe it was a trick. And where was Angela? Theo could only hope that she was safe and hiding somewhere where Scott wouldn't find her.

"*Do* something…" Theo muttered to himself.

But what? Scott might be hiding somewhere behind one of the pillars in the basement, just waiting for him. But on the other hand, maybe Scott had left the basement and was entering the shaft from another entrance, trying to cut him off. Theo looked around again. How could he get down without breaking his neck? A fat lot of use he'd be to Ricky then. The table was underneath the shaft but it looked a long way down. A very long way down.

Theo swallowed hard. Jump… That was easier said than done, but he couldn't hang about in the shaft all day, especially with Scott after him. Theo curled himself up into a ball, manoeuvring so that his feet were under him. He leaned back, kicking his legs out before him so that they dangled out of the shaft. Then he sat up, his legs dangling out over the wall, but now came the hard part. Theo took a deep breath and held it. He swivelled the top part of his body and kicked off with his legs, letting his feet slap into the wall to absorb the impact before the rest of his body. He now dangled down from the tunnel, facing the wall with only his fingertips holding him up – and his arms were already aching.

Theo pushed off with his hands. Barely a second passed before he made contact with the table. He bent his knees the way he'd been taught in PE but a shock like lightning zapped up his right leg. Theo grimaced and slid down off the table. The moment his right foot touched the floor, pain like nothing he had ever felt before flamed through his leg. He dropped to the floor, clutching his foot. Beads of perspiration dampened his forehead and trickled down his back. The basement started to swim around him. The light rocked back and forth, growing more and more dim.

"Don't pass out. Don't you dare pass out," Theo muttered, fighting down the waves of nausea that threatened to overwhelm him.

He had to get up. He had to *move* before Scott caught him. Most people already thought he was pretty feeble. Was he going to prove them right or wrong now? Theo struggled to his feet. He touched his right foot down on to the ground. Sharp, intense pain speared through his leg again. His mouth filled with cool saliva, which he swallowed convulsively. He had to get out of there. Gritting his teeth, Theo hopped towards the exit doors at the far side of the basement. With a little luck, Scott would be busy searching for him in the tun…

The exit doors burst open. Scott stood stock still, filling the doorway. He took a step forwards. Theo took a step backwards, never taking his eyes off the man before him. Scott took another step forwards. Theo took another step back. It was like some strange dance between the two of them. Then Scott broke into a run. Theo turned, stumbling, before he picked himself up and pelted towards the shaft. The pain in his ankle was distant, low down on the list of his current priorities. His heart hammered and his blood roared in his ears. But where was he running to? There was nowhere to go. The entrance of the shaft was far too high to get to, even if he managed to jump up on to the table. He'd just have to… But Theo got no further.

In the next moment, he found himself swept off his feet. He lashed out, flailing with his feet, his elbows, hitting backwards with his head. Scott groaned and swore viciously, but his arms were like a vice around Theo's chest.

"Let me go! LET ME GO!" Theo shouted, struggling harder.

Scott held him up higher, his arms wrapped

around Theo's chest in a bear hug. Theo's feet were a good thirty centimetres off the ground. In amongst all the panic and fear, Theo felt the pain of his ribs being squeezed tight. He had to *do* something – before Scott broke all his ribs, before he passed out. Theo stretched his legs out in front of him, until they were almost at right angles with the rest of his body. Then he bent his head and bit as hard as he could into Scott's arm, kicking back with his legs at the same time. As Theo's heels made hard contact with Scott's shins, Theo ignored the pain dancing in his ankle and kicked back again, biting down harder into Scott's forearm.

"Oww!" Scott hollered, dropping Theo to the floor.

Theo sprang up immediately, ready to leg it, when he heard a clunk and a crash, followed by the sound of wood splintering. He turned and leapt to one side – just in time. Scott hit the floor like a felled tree. And there behind him stood Angela, still holding what was left of the wooden chair she'd applied to Scott's back and head. Her face was paper white as she stared down at Scott.

"Is … is he dead?" Angela whispered.

Theo squatted down and cautiously felt Scott's wrist. "I can feel his pulse beat – and he's still breathing," he replied at last.

Angela breathed a huge sigh of relief. Only then did she realize that she was still holding what was left of the chair. She dropped it as if it was suddenly burning her hands.

"We'd better tie him up before he wakes up," Theo decided.

"Do we have to?" Angela backed away.

"I think so. It'd be safer. You look through the holdall, I'll keep an eye on him," Theo said. "Oh, and Angela?"

"Yeah?"

"Thanks!"

"You'd do the same for me," Angela shrugged. And she and Theo smiled at each other.

Minutes later, Scott's feet were bound and his hands were securely tied behind his back using some stout rope from his own holdall. And in all that time he hadn't moved a muscle.

"Will he be all right, d'you think?" Angela asked.

"Yeah, of course. Anyway, who cares?!" Theo dismissed. He had a lot more on his mind than some criminal scuzbucket who'd tried to separate his head from his body. "Did you find Ricky? Is he somewhere else in this building?"

Angela shook her head. "I didn't get the chance to search properly. I was having a hunt around when I heard you shout something about hoping someone had cracked their head. I reckoned I should duck down and keep out of sight after that."

"OK then. Let's search this place from top to bottom," Theo suggested. He took another look at Scott. "We should gag him first."

Theo took out the hankie that Mum had insisted he carry with him until he was totally over his cold and twirled it around until it was a thick cord of none-too-clean material.

Squatting down, he pulled it between Scott's teeth and tied it in a double knot at the back of his head.

"And stay there!" he ordered the still unconscious body.

He and Angela set off towards the exit, but Theo had barely taken a step when his ankle made its presence felt. He winced, immediately raising his right foot off the floor.

"What's the matter?" asked Angela.

"I did something to my ankle when I jumped down from the ventilator shaft," Theo explained.

"Is it broken?"

"I don't know. I don't think so," Theo said doubtfully. When Scott had chased him, he'd still managed to use it so it couldn't be broken. Mind you, his adrenalin level must've been off the scale so maybe he just couldn't feel it then.

"Wait here. I'll go and have a look," said Angela.

"But…"

"You can't do much with a bad foot.

Besides, you'd only slow me down," Angela pointed out.

She didn't even wait for Theo to reply, before running off.

Theo watched her go, his lips a hard line across his face. Angela had no right to treat him like a spare tyre, like he was totally useless. Why did people always do that? It was as if everyone in the universe only remembered his name when they wanted something from him. Otherwise he didn't exist. He was always one of the last to get picked when sides were being chosen for football. When he put his hand up in class to answer a question, he practically had to jump up and down on his desk before Mrs Daltry even knew he was there. The only sure way he could get her attention was to have a cold and sneeze all over her. Everyone ignored him – except Ricky. Ricky didn't think he was a waste of space...

Theo waited and waited, gently twisting his foot first one way, then the other. It wasn't too bad now.

Time passed. Where was she? Theo didn't

hear a sound from anywhere in the warehouse.

"You idiot!" he suddenly hissed to himself.

Angela was probably out of the warehouse and well on her way to warning her brother by this time.

But she couldn't. She *wouldn't*. She knocked Scott out, Theo reminded himself.

So what? All Angela cared about was her brother. And she certainly wasn't going to let Theo mess things up for Tom and herself.

"Angela?" Theo hobbled forward. "ANGELA?"

No reply. She was obviously long gone. But what had Theo expected?

"Moron!" Theo berated himself through gritted teeth.

Now what? Angela had gone. And where was Ricky? He'd failed again…

17 THE IRVING MUSEUM

Behind him, Scott groaned. Theo turned. Scott was still lying on his stomach, his hands behind his back. He raised his head and shook it, as if to clear it. Theo instinctively backed away, ignoring the sudden sharp pain in his ankle. Scott turned his head, his eyes chips of ice when he saw Theo.

"Llmm … m … ou … plem…" What he lacked in coherence, Scott made up for in volume.

Theo increased the distance between the two of them. Scott tried to crawl like a caterpillar towards Theo, but gave up after moving only a few centimetres. Even though Theo couldn't make out what he was saying, there was no mistaking the blazing fury in his eyes or the tension which kept his whole body rigid.

"Llmm … m … ou … ymm … toa…"

"The same to you, mate!" Theo replied.

He turned and hobbled to the door. Surprisingly, with each step, the pain was growing slightly easier. He opened the door and hopped out into the small hall. There were toilets on the left and a staircase leading up to the ground floor on the right.

"ANGELA…?" Theo tried again.

"What's the matter?" Angela called from the top of the stairs. "Ricky's not here. Robbie must have taken Ricky with him when we were still in the ventilator shaft."

"So what do we do now?" Theo asked.

"No police. Not yet," Angela said quickly. "I don't want my brother to get into trouble."

"Isn't it a bit late for that?" Theo asked.

Angela shook her head. "Not necessarily. Once Tom sees that Robbie decided to use Ricky as a hostage after all, he might see sense."

"I'm fed up waiting for your brother to

grow a brain," said Theo with contempt. "This job – whatever it is – is going to happen at the local museum so I think we..."

"Museum?" Angela interrupted.

"Before Robbie left the warehouse he told Scott not to be late to the Irving. The only Irving around here is the Irving Museum," Theo explained.

"Of course!" Angela breathed. "That explains those drawings I saw."

"What drawings?"

"I'll explain when we get there. Theo, we can do this. We don't need anyone else. We can get Ricky and Tom out of there." An uncomfortable pause followed as Theo considered his next move. "Theo, are you coming with me?"

"What d'you think?" Theo replied, his voice hard. But uncertainty gnawed at him like a hungry dog with a bone.

Angela nodded, relieved. Theo wriggled his ankle again. It didn't feel too bad now. He could only hope that it would last out until Ricky was safe. Theo glanced at Angela. If it came down to a choice between saving her brother or saving Ricky, which one would she choose? Theo slowly shook his head. No contest...

"Let's go. We don't have much time," Angela said.

"Lead the way," Theo replied. "I'm right behind you."

Where you can't stab me in the back! Theo kept that bit to himself.

As they walked up the stairs, Theo wondered out loud, "I wonder what they intend to do at the museum?"

He turned to Angela. The light of realization was on her face too.

"The Greek and Roman jewellery collection... Of course."

There was meant to be a school trip to the Irving Museum on Friday but if Robbie and his friends got their way, there would be nothing left to see!

"I don't understand. That collection must be guarded night and day. How do they hope to get away with it?" Theo asked.

"They've got someone on the inside working for them," Angela admitted.

"Who?"

"The security guard. My brother Tom is a security guard there…"

Theo stared in amazement. Talk about setting a wolf to watch the sheep!

He shook his head. "I don't like this – not one little bit. This is getting more and more dangerous, Angela. We should phone the police."

"When we've got Ricky and my brother out of there. We can't call them until then," Angela insisted.

"We should phone them now. We might not get another chance," Theo replied.

"What d'you mean?"

"Robbie had a gun – I saw it. For all we know, your brother and that other guy Dylan could have guns as well. Someone could end up hurt – or killed."

"Tom won't let that happen," Angela said firmly.

There it was again – that total faith in her

brother. She just couldn't bear to hear anything said against Tom. It was as if Theo's words entered her ears but couldn't get to her brain. Theo gritted his teeth with frustration. It was decision time.

"Sorry, Angela, but I think it's best to call the police. Tom and the others are all in the one place now. The police can handle it from here."

"You can't do that…"

"I've got no choice." Theo turned to walk away.

"If you go to the police, I'll phone my brother on his mobile and warn him that the police are coming," Angela called after him. "Tom, Ricky and the others will be long gone by the time the police get there."

Stunned, Theo turned back to Angela. "You'd do that?" he whispered.

"If you don't leave me any choice – yes," Angela said through thinned lips.

"Well, now we both know where we stand, don't we?" Theo said quietly.

"Yes, we do."

Silence.

"All right, we'll play it your way. But I'm warning you, Angela. I'll go to the museum with you but that's it. If anything goes wrong, if we don't get Ricky out, I'm going to call the police and nothing you can say will stop me," Theo said.

Angela frowned at him.

"I mean it," Theo said, his voice quiet.

"OK. OK." Angela nodded reluctantly. "What about Scott?"

"What about him?" Theo dismissed. "As soon as we get Ricky, we'll phone the police and tell them where to find him."

They left the warehouse by the front gate and set off.

"How do we get into the museum?" Theo asked.

His ankle was making him limp slightly but the pain was bearable.

"The same way Tom and the others will – using the delivery entrance."

At Theo's thoughtful look Angela added reluctantly, "I heard Scott talking about it when I climbed down from my bedroom."

"I see," said Theo. "And how're you going to get your brother out of there without alerting the others?"

"You leave that to me," Angela replied.

"OK then. Tell me how we get Ricky out of there when we know that at least Robbie has a gun?" said Theo.

Angela frowned. "That's a bit more tricky. But we'll think of something!"

"I'm glad you think so," sniffed Theo.

Fifteen minutes later they both stood before the Irving Museum. The evening was still light and bright with hardly a cloud in the sky. Theo looked around. There were still quite a few people milling about. He turned back to the museum. The Irving was the biggest museum in the town. Mrs Daltry always saw to it that her class visited the museum at least once a year. Theo didn't think it was too bad. There were always plenty of experiments that you could do by yourself – always plenty of buttons to press, and levers to pull and plenty of gadgets to put together. And the exhibition of Greek and Roman jewellery was one of the biggest exhibitions the Irving had ever staged. What had Mrs Daltry called the collection? Priceless?

How did Robbie and the rest plan to rob the museum? Theo would've thought there'd be more than just one security guard looking after all that priceless ancient jewellery. He'd leave it to the police to figure out how Robbie and the others planned to do it. Right now, all he was concerned about was Ricky.

Angela glanced at her watch. "It's past seven. The museum has been shut for over an hour."

"D'you think they're in there?"

"They must be. They're probably wondering what happened to Scott," Angela replied.

Theo looked up at the imposing building with its high colonnades and its huge double-doored entrance. It would've been so wonderful to have X-ray vision. Theo didn't really fancy blundering into the museum and getting caught before he'd even taken two steps. What were Robbie and Dylan and Tom doing at that precise moment?

"This way," Angela said, whispering even though they were several metres away from the museum.

Without a word, Theo followed her. Angela veered off to the right and turned the corner to walk down the side of the building.

"D'you know where you're going?" Theo asked.

Angela looked back at him and sheepishly shook her head. "Not exactly."

"That's what I thought!" said Theo, ruefully.

"The delivery entrance must be around here somewhere," Angela mused.

They walked all the way around the building, which occupied the entire block. There were plenty of doors around the block which looked likely but there was only one problem – they were all locked.

"You're sure…"

"Yes," Angela snapped before Theo could get any further. "Listen, I know you don't trust me and I suppose in your shoes I wouldn't trust me either! But I told you the truth. Tom was going to enter the museum as normal and then open the delivery door for them. That's all I know."

"Why can't the others go through the same entrance as Tom?" asked Theo.

"Because all the ways into the museum – except the delivery entrance – have close-circuit TV cameras monitoring them. Everyone who enters or leaves the building is taped," Angela explained.

"So where is this delivery entrance?"

Angela looked up and down the main street, perplexed. "Wait a minute… Across the street… I remember now. I overheard Dylan say something about a long corridor in the basement leading to the ground floor. He was complaining that he only had ninety seconds to run one hundred metres, deactivate some special alarm and knock out the close-circuit monitors before all the bells went off. Tom couldn't do that bit for some reason. It needs an electronics expert."

"One hundred metres? But that's well into the next block on every side," Theo pointed out.

"The delivery door must be in one of the other blocks then," said Angela.

"We'll be here all night," Theo complained. "And suppose we still can't find the entrance?"

"I'm all ears if you've got any better suggestions," Angela frowned.

"All right. Let's try that block first," said Theo, pointing to the next block across the street on the right.

Theo and Angela crossed over the road and started looking.

"I would've thought the delivery entrance would be quite big," Theo thought out loud.

"Maybe. But don't forget the front doors are huge as well."

"Even so."

They examined every door they passed, particularly those that weren't attached to shops. Turning first one corner, then another, then the last one in the block, it looked like they were going to be unsuccessful when Theo spotted a huge set of doors with no number on them and no shops on either side.

"Angela, look," Theo pointed.

They both ran up to the doors and studied them hard. The doors were high and made of wood painted black, with a huge door knob on each. There was no bell or knocker on or beside them. Nothing which indicated how you got someone on the inside to open them.

"What d'you think?" Theo asked.

Angela shrugged. "Could be…"

They looked at each other.

"Go on then," urged Angela.

"Last chance to call the police?" Theo tried.

"No," Angela replied vehemently.

Slowly, Theo stretched out his hand towards the doors. That hot, queasy, uneasy feeling in the pit of his stomach was back.

"Oh, let me," Angela said impatiently.

She pushed at one of the double doors as hard as she could, then the other. Nothing happened. Angela tried harder, groaning at the effort. Still nothing.

"It's no good." She straightened up, panting. "The doors won't budge. We'll have to think of something else."

Theo frowned stubbornly. He wasn't going to turn back now. No way. He looked up and down the huge double doors, then at the door knobs. Stretching out his hand, he grasped one door knob and pulled it towards him. The door opened easily and silently. Theo turned to look at Angela, his eyebrows raised.

"OK! OK! Don't rub it in!" said Angela.

Theo looked past the doors. The darkness inside spilt out on to the pavement. He took a tentative step forward. There was a lift and some stairs but that was it. No corridors, no rooms, nothing else.

"This must be it," Theo said doubtfully.

He stepped inside. It was immediately cooler and quieter. In the space of a couple of steps, the traffic noises outside all but disappeared, even though the door was still partially opened.

"Well? Aren't you coming?" Theo asked Angela.

With extreme reluctance, Angela followed Theo inside. As the door swung shut, Theo said quickly, "Don't let it slam."

Angela caught the door just in time. A centimetre at a time, she let it close with a faint click. Theo and Angela walked over to the lift. Angela reached out to press the button when Theo caught her hand.

"No," he said, shaking his head. "I think we should take the stairs. Someone might hear the lift moving. We don't want anyone to know we're here."

As there was a staircase leading down to basement level and no other staircase leading up beyond the ground floor, Theo and Angela walked down the steps side by side. The stairs were grouped in sets of ten before they levelled off and started down again in a spiral.

"I can't hear anything," Angela whispered.

"Neither can I."

After Theo and Angela had walked down for at least two minutes, the stairs finally stopped. They were in some kind of storage area. Mummy cases, display cases, odd bits of PCs, a cross section of a small plane leaning against a high wall, a strange looking engine, a two–metre–high model of an eye – as Theo looked around he felt like Ali Baba in a cave of treasures. Assorted items were scattered here, there and everywhere but with a definite gap leading through them, forming a corridor.

"At least we know we're in the right place," Theo whispered. "This is a lot more interesting than the museum itself."

"Come on," Angela beckoned. "The museum must be that way."

Weaving their way through the strange items, Theo and Angela made their way along the corridor. Theo looked around this way and that, keeping his eyes and ears as wide open as possible. He wanted to find Ricky, not any of the others. Angela's brother Tom was robbing the museum along with the rest of his gang and as far as Theo was concerned, that made him just as dangerous.

"We must be underneath the street," said Angela, looking up.

Theo looked up and listened. He couldn't hear a thing, even though there had to be traffic roaring over them. They carried on walking to the far end of the corridor. There was another lift and another set of stairs. The echo of a distant, rhythmic knocking filled the air. Theo put his fingers over his lips and pointed to the stairs. Angela nodded. They both crept up the concrete stairs on tiptoe, their steps slowing the further up the staircase they got. The knocking grew louder and louder.

Theo was scared. He admitted it to himself and felt strangely better for it. He was close to Ricky – he could feel it, and he was scared.

At the top of the staircase, there was another lift entrance and a set of double doors. They tiptoed over to the doors. Theo listened hard, then pushed one open very, very slowly. He peeked out, then carefully let it shut again.

"We're on the ground floor of the museum," he whispered. "Where's the Astral Collection being held? Which floor?"

"No idea. Ask me another," Angela whispered back.

"There's three of them, plus your brother, plus Ricky – so we'll have to be very careful and fifteen-sixteenths," Theo said. "There might be other guards in the museum working with them for all we know."

"I don't think so."

"Well, we can't take any chances."

"Should we split up?" Angela asked.

Theo looked at her. "I don't think so. I think it'd be safer if we stuck together."

Angela regarded him steadily. "You don't trust me, do you? What d'you think I'm going to do? Run off and warn them."

"I never said that."

"But that's what you meant…"

"Can we discuss this once we've got Ricky out of here?" Theo asked, exasperated.

"Ricky and my brother," Angela reminded him.

"Hhmm!" was all Theo said.

He listened at the door again, then pushed it open a fraction to peep outside again. Nodding to Angela, he crept out as if he was walking through a graveyard at night. Angela quickly followed him. They ducked down behind the nearest display case and listened. Theo tried to focus in on the knocking sound which echoed almost eerily all around them. It was definitely coming from somewhere on the ground floor but the museum was filled with ante-rooms and alcoves leading off the main hall which could disguise where the noise was really coming from.

"Think!" Theo muttered sternly.

He'd been to the museum before on many occasions – so think! The Astral Collection… Where would they put a big, important display like that? Of course! The Irving Room. Where else? Whenever the museum put on an important exhibition like – what had it been last year? – The Chinese Terracotta Army – then they always put it in the Irving Room towards the back of the museum.

"This way," Theo whispered.

"Where're we going?" asked Angela, anxiously.

"The Irving Room."

Theo didn't give Angela a chance to ask any more. He didn't want to stop or slow down for too long. That gave him too much opportunity to ask himself just what on earth he thought he was doing! Crawling on his hands and knees, Theo made his way towards the back of the museum. Behind him, Angela made scuffling noises as she followed him. Theo turned his head to glare at her.

"Sorry!" Angela mouthed.

They carried on moving, scurrying from display case to display case until, from round the side of a case, Theo could see the entrance of the Irving Room only a couple of metres away. And that's not all he could see.

Ricky was there. He was sitting down outside the entrance to the Irving Room. He was tied up like a supermarket chicken, with his hands tied behind his back, his feet bound and a big piece of sticky plaster covering his mouth. But it was definitely Ricky.

Excited, Theo opened his mouth to call out to him, only remembering where he was when he heard the loud knocking sound again. Then Theo really saw Ricky, really took in his appearance for the first time.

Ricky looked terrible.

There were streaks running down his face

from his eyes which were red and sore. Ricky had been crying – a lot. His eyes were cast down and he looked so miserable and lonely and frightened that Theo felt anger rising up in him – and it was far stronger than the fear he felt.

Cautiously, he raised his head above the display case and looked around. The main display hall where he and Angela were hiding seemed to be all clear but there was some definite activity in the Irving Room. Theo ducked back down behind the display case.

"Wait here." Without giving Angela time to argue, Theo crept out from behind the display case and raced for the wall adjacent to the Irving Room where there was no cover. If one of the thieves came out now, he'd be caught for sure. Squatting down, Theo took another look around. He had to find some way of untying Ricky and getting him out of the museum without the others seeing. The problem was, Theo was on one side of the entrance to the Irving Room and Ricky was on the other.

"Psssst! Psssst!" Theo couldn't risk saying it any louder in case he was overheard. "Pssssst!"

Ricky looked up. His eyes widened with shock and surprise.

"Umm… The… Ge…" Ricky struggled to sit up, nodding in the direction of the Irving Room.

Frantically, Theo shook his head, putting his finger over his lips.

"The… ru…" Ricky struggled harder against the ropes that bound his hands and feet.

"I thought you tied that boy up and gagged him?" said an angry voice.

"I did," another man protested.

"Go and see what's the matter with him," the first voice ordered from inside the Irving Room.

Footsteps sounded on the wooden floor, getting closer and closer. Theo looked desperately at the nearest display case. There was no way he could run back to it without being seen. The footsteps were almost out of the room. Theo crouched down lower against the wall, knowing with absolute certainty that he was going to be caught...

18 CHOICES

"**D**ylan, it's me." Angela stood up and ran over to the entrance of the Irving Room.

She stood between Theo and the entrance, just as a man whom Theo couldn't see came out into the main hall. Theo made himself as small as possible, crouching down against the wall. If he could've merged with it, he would have. He didn't dare blink, he didn't dare breathe. His heart was pounding so loudly, surely it could be heard throughout the entire museum?

"Angela! What the hell are you doing here?" Dylan exclaimed. "Tom, it's your sister."

Theo stared at Dylan's shoes, visible just past Angela's legs. He couldn't bring himself to look up. If he didn't look in Dylan's direction, maybe Dylan wouldn't look in his. Angela put one hand behind her and waved at Theo to stay back. Another set of footsteps sounded on the floor. An arm emerged and pulled Angela into the Irving Room. Theo crept forward slowly, still holding his breath.

"Angela, what're you doing here? And this had better be good." The low, deep voice held quiet menace.

"Robbie, I... I wanted to make sure that Tom was all right..." Angela's voice trailed off into a miserable silence.

"Angela, you shouldn't have come here. I'm fine."

Theo peeped around the corner. Tom was looking worriedly from Robbie to Angela and back again.

"Tom's right. You shouldn't have come here," said Robbie. There was more in his voice than just agreement with Tom. Nervously, Tom moved to stand nearer to his sister. Angela was the only one directly facing the entrance. The others were too busy glaring at her. Theo caught Angela's eye. They both knew she was in deep trouble. Angela looked up at her brother, so as not to give Theo away. Theo had to act NOW. Summoning up all the courage he possessed, Theo raced across the entrance, keeping low and on tiptoe. He flung himself against the wall as soon as he was clear of the entrance and waited.

"Robbie, listen. It's not a problem," Tom said earnestly. "I'll take care of her. I'll make sure she stays out of our way."

"Angela, how did you know where we were?" Robbie asked. There was no mistaking the menace in his voice.

"I listened when you were all in our kitchen," Angela admitted. "That's how I knew how to get in."

Theo stepped behind Ricky and bent down to try and untie his hands and feet.

"Shush…" Theo whispered softly in his friend's ear.

"And where's Scott? He should've been here by now," said Robbie.

"How s-should I know where he is?" Angela tried and failed to keep her voice steady.

"What's going on, Angela?" Robbie's voice was even softer than before.

Theo's fingers had all turned into thumbs and the knots felt like they'd been superglued in place. At last they began to give. Moments later, Ricky's hands were free. Ricky pulled the tape off his face, suppressing a wince of pain as he did so. Then he quickly untied his feet.

"There's nothing going on," Angela replied. "I told you, I just wanted to be with Tom. I've got to look out for him. You lot sure won't."

Theo pointed towards the nearest display case in the main hall and the ante-room behind it. Ricky nodded, understanding. Ricky got to his feet and they both dashed for the display case. Theo turned back to see what was going on in the Irving Room.

"I'm tired of falling over kids every time I turn around," Robbie said.

"Calm down, Robbie," Dylan soothed. "That boy was just an accident. And Angela is Tom's sister. We can trust her. She wouldn't betray us."

"You reckon?" Robbie chided. "I wouldn't trust that girl to spit on me if I was on fire."

"You got that right!" Angela replied, frost in her voice.

"Angela! You're not helping," Tom pleaded.

Theo indicated the next case down and he and Ricky made a dash for it. Theo wanted to put as much distance as possible between them and Robbie but really they needed to be on the other side of the main hall where the exit to the basement was. The problem was how to get there. Robbie and Dylan were now standing side on to the Irving Room entrance. If Theo and Ricky risked darting across the hall, they'd be spotted for sure. And besides, Theo didn't want to leave Angela behind with that lot. If she hadn't come out into the open like that, he'd have been caught for sure. He had to admit, Angela was brave if nothing else.

"What's going on? What's Angela doing here?" Ricky frowned. "How come she knows all of them?"

"Tom, the one with the dark brown hair, is her brother," Theo explained.

"Her *brother*?" Ricky said, aghast.

"Yeah. Shush! I'll explain later."

Theo looked around. He had to get himself, Ricky and Angela out of there in a hurry. But how?

How?

A diversion. He needed a diversion.

"Ricky, listen," Theo whispered quickly. "See the door behind that display case?" he pointed across the hall.

"Yeah?"

"There's a staircase and a lift beyond that door which lead down to a basement corridor. You've got to get to the other end of that corridor and up the stairs on the other side. That'll take you out into the street on the opposite side of the museum. Then leg it to the nearest phone box and phone for the police."

"What about you?"

"Don't worry about me. I'm going to run interference for you."

"Huh?"

"I'm going to create a diversion. Wait until the coast is clear, then make a run for it," Theo said.

"But Theo, Robbie's got a gun. You can't outrun a bullet," Ricky exclaimed.

"D'you know if any of the others have guns?"

"No, they don't. Just Robbie."

"OK then," Theo said grimly. "I'm still gonna go for it."

"But Theo…"

"Ricky, we've got no choice," Theo countered.

"Angela, if you've done anything, *anything* to mess up my plans…" Robbie took a step closer to Angela, who immediately backed away from him.

"Watch out, Angela," Dylan said quickly. "Don't touch those cases. I haven't deactivated the alarms on them yet."

Angela turned to look at the Astral Collection, sparkling in the five display cases behind her. She took a step towards them. Robbie leapt forward and grabbed her by the arm.

"Oh, no, you don't," he hissed.

"Ow! You're hurting me," Angela protested, trying to prise his fingers off her upper arm.

"Robbie, let her go." Tom tried to pull Robbie away from his sister. Robbie turned and, without letting go of Angela, he pushed Tom away from him.

"It's now or never," Theo whispered to Ricky. "Duck down and keep out of sight until you can make a break for it."

"OK," Ricky replied doubtfully. "And Theo?"

"Yes?"

"Am I glad to see you!"

It took a moment for what Ricky had said to sink in.

"What're friends for?" Theo smiled ruefully.

Without further delay, Theo made his way on all fours down the hall, using the display cases as cover. At the end of the hall, he raced up the stairs to the first floor, keeping close to the wall. On the landing he picked up a blue and white pottery vase off a plinth and ran along to stand just above the Irving Room. Theo held out the vase over the banister, striving to keep his arms out – at least for the moment.

"Oi! I know you're there and I'm going to call the police," Theo shouted out.

"What the hell…?"

Theo heard footsteps charging out of the Irving Room. The moment he saw a head below him, he released the vase. He didn't miss, either! Dylan was just looking up when the vase cracked him on the top of his head. He crumpled up like wet newspaper and was out like a light. On impact, the vase shattered into a thousand pieces which rained down around him.

"I hope that vase wasn't expensive," Theo murmured.

Tom emerged from the Irving Room, followed by Robbie who was still holding a struggling Angela in his vice-like grip. Frantically, Theo hunted around for something else to drop, but it was too late. Tom and Robbie had seen him. They both jumped forward, already out of the range of anything else Theo might drop.

"Go and get him," Robbie ordered Tom.

Theo stared down in frustrated panic. This wouldn't work if Robbie didn't come after him as well. Robbie looked up at Theo. His green, cat-like eyes narrowed. Already Tom was running down the main hall on his way to the stairs.

"Angela – RUN!" Theo shouted.

Angela didn't need to be told twice. She gave Robbie a kick in the shins that Theo felt from up on the first floor. Robbie yelped and released her immediately, clutching his leg. Angela took off like a bolt from a crossbow towards the door where she and Theo had come in.

Time to follow her example, Theo decided.

Tom was on the stairs and gaining fast. Theo ran along the upstairs landing, darting into a large room off the walkway. This room was full of pictures and models of dinosaurs. Various display cases were filled with dinosaur paraphernalia. This had always been one of Theo's favourite rooms but now was not the time to relax and enjoy it!

"Angela, take one more step and I'll shoot. Your choice," Robbie's voice froze Theo in his tracks.

Robbie was going to shoot Angela. He was actually going to shoot her...

"Robbie, don't," Tom called out from the first-floor landing. At the sound of Tom's retreating footsteps, Theo ran out of the dinosaur room, edging along the landing until he could see down into the main hall. Robbie was holding a gun and pointing it straight at Angela who stared at him, horror-stricken.

"Robbie, no! Don't!" Tom charged down the stairs and ran towards Robbie, stopping only when Robbie turned to point the gun at him.

Theo ran silently along the landing and

down the stairs, careful to keep to the wall and out of sight.

"Robbie, calm down," Tom soothed. "It's only my sister."

"She kicked me," Robbie hissed.

"You probably frightened her." Tom shrugged with careful nonchalance. "You know she's got a bit of a temper. But she can be trusted. She'd never do anything to hurt me, to hurt us."

"No? Then why am I up to my armpits in kids? Where did that boy Ricky come from?" Robbie nodded in the direction of the Irving Room. "And where ... did...?" Robbie's voice trailed off as he realized Ricky was no longer by the entrance. Eyes blazing with rage, he turned back to Angela who recoiled from his look as if it was a physical slap. There came a loud click as Robbie drew back the hammer on his revolver.

"Where is he, Angela?" he asked.

"I don't know. I swear I don't. I didn't let him go..."

Robbie took a step towards her. Tom ran to

stand between his sister and Robbie.

"Robbie, listen to me. We can still do this. We can still take the jewels and blow." Tom spoke rapidly. "Ricky and my sister aren't the important ones now. The Astral Collection is. And it's *ours*. Robbie, listen!"

"Get out of the way, Tom."

"No way."

"Tom, move," Robbie demanded.

Tom straightened up slowly. "No, Robbie. She's my sister. I'm not going to let you hurt my sister."

Robbie and Tom studied each other for a long, tortuous moment.

"Ricky, I know you're here somewhere," Robbie called out, his eyes never leaving Tom's. "You've got five seconds to show yourself otherwise I shoot Tom and his sister and then I'm coming after you. Five... Four..."

Theo could hardly breathe. What should he do? He crawled along the floor towards Ricky who was still crouched behind a display case. So much for his so-called plan. Everything was falling apart, crumbling around him.

"Three…"

From the sound of it, Robbie had gone off the deep end. There was no way Robbie would let any of them leave the museum alive to grass on him. Theo knew that as surely as he knew his own name.

"Two…"

"All right! All right! I'm here." Ricky stood up quickly before Theo could reach him.

"And the other boy…" Robbie called out. "You can come out too or your friends get it. And this time I'm not even gonna count."

Think … *think*… Theo had to think of something, *fast*.

The display cases…

"Show yourself. I'm not going to ask you a third time…" Robbie warned.

Theo stood up immediately.

"Now all of you. In there." Robbie indicated the Irving Room with his gun.

Reluctantly Theo followed the others into the Irving Room with Robbie entering the room last. Theo briefly thought about launching himself at Robbie, but he dismissed the notion at once.

Don't be a doof! he thought.

Robbie would shoot him before he'd taken two steps. And no way could he outrun a bullet. Robbie's gun was very real. Not a toy, not filled with blanks but with real bullets that could kill and maim. And Robbie wasn't playing games. The man was already several sandwiches short of a picnic. They all had to be really careful now. Anything might set him off.

"Robbie, look. The jewels are here." Tom pointed with a smile. "Don't lose sight of what we came here for."

"Shut up. Just shut up," Robbie roared. "Everything's gone wrong and it's all your fault. You and your sister. Look at this. Three kids. Count 'em. Three! Scott's missing and Dylan's unconscious." He pointed his gun at Theo. "I ought to do you for that alone…"

Theo took a small, terrified step backwards. His mouth dried instantly. Sweat trickled down his back like rain on a window-pane. He didn't, *couldn't* take his eyes off Robbie.

"You can wake up Dylan. And Scott's probably just been delayed," Tom said calmly.

"If anything's happened to Scott, anything at all..." Robbie threatened.

Theo could feel Angela look at him but he was careful not to look back... That would give them away for sure.

"Robbie, that gun you're holding is the only thing stopping us from leaving here rich and free. If we tie up Ricky and the other one, by the time they're found we'll be long gone. Think about it."

Robbie frowned at Tom. "Dylan's our alarm expert. How do we get at the jewels without triggering the alarm?"

"Wake Dylan up!" Tom said as if it was the most obvious thing in the world.

"Tom..." Angela began.

"Shut up and stay out of this, Angela," Tom said harshly.

Angela's mouth snapped shut.

"OK then. I'll bring Dylan around," Robbie said at last. "You kids stand against that wall and don't move, unless you want your next move to be your last."

Theo, Ricky and Angela stepped back against the wall at once. They had no choice with Robbie pointing his gun at them.

"That's more like it. Let's get to it, Robbie," Tom grinned.

"Hhmm!" Robbie turned around and walked towards Dylan.

Without warning, Tom sprang at him, knocking him to the ground. The gun flew out of Robbie's hand and went off as it hit the ground, shooting into the main hall. Then everything happened at once. Robbie twisted like a snake shedding its skin and punched Tom viciously on the side of his face. Angela raced forward, trying to dodge past the two men on the floor. Theo picked up the security guard's chair next to him and, leaping forward, he smashed it down on the nearest display case. The glass shattered and flew in all directions. Theo dropped the chair immediately to shield his face and eyes from the glass. Instantly an ear-splitting klaxon sounded throughout the museum. Ricky jumped over the two men still trading blows on the floor and raced off like the wind. Robbie kicked Tom off him and launched himself towards the gun.

But Angela got there first.

"Give me the gun, Angela," Robbie ordered, jumping to his feet.

"Stay where you are." Angela had to shout over the noise of the klaxon.

Tom sprang to his feet, wiping the blood trickling from his nose on the back of his hand. He moved forward, past Robbie towards his sister.

"Well done, Angela. Now give me the gun," he smiled.

"Angela." Theo ran over to stand beside her. "Don't give it to either of them."

"D'you want it?" Angela asked.

"No fear," Theo replied immediately. No way did he even want to touch the thing. It was giving him chills just being this close to it. "Just don't give it to those two either."

"Angela, don't listen to him. I'm your brother. Give it to me," Tom said, incredulously.

"There's no way I'm going to let you hand over my property to your brother," Robbie threatened.

Angela took a step back, looking from her brother to Robbie and back again. She cupped her left hand under her right to steady it, pointing the gun in both Robbie's and Tom's direction. The gun visibly shook in her hand.

Theo felt he should do something, anything but he didn't know what. He could see the fearful indecision all over Angela's face. But it was up to her now. She had the gun and it was her choice.

19 FAMILY LOYALTY

Angela glanced down at the gun. She flicked a tiny switch at the side of it and the chamber fell to one side. Tipping up the gun she let the bullets fall into her hand.

"Theo, lose those," she said, handing them over.

"Angela, you fool," Tom shouted.

Robbie leapt forward towards her, rage like nothing Theo had ever seen all over his face. Tom rugby-tackled him to the ground and they were at it again. Theo backed off fast, pulling Angela back with him, in case Robbie should win this bout.

"Let's get out of here," Theo suggested.

"No, I can't. Tom might need me." Angela pulled away from him.

"Then let's get the police. We can't handle Robbie. He's a nutter! He probably drinks blood and sleeps hanging upside down from a tree."

"I'm not leaving my brother," Angela insisted.

Theo scowled at her. If she didn't leave her brother, then he couldn't leave her. He looked around for Ricky but there was no sign of him. He looked back at Robbie and Tom. They weren't having a boxing match like on the telly. They were punching and gouging and using their whole bodies to hurt each other. It was vicious and nasty and made Theo feel sick.

"Do something," Angela implored him.

"Like what?" Theo asked.

"I don't know. *Do* something. Robbie's going to kill him."

Bewildered, Theo looked around for something he could use. Then he saw a fire hose tucked away in the corner to his right.

Maybe he could just douse the two of them. The water in fire hoses came out at quite some pressure. That should be enough to separate the two men.

Then they'll both be cheesed off with you rather than each other! Theo thought.

But he didn't have much choice. Angela was looking at him, expecting him to do something. Theo ran over to the glass-fronted cabinet which housed the fire hose. It was locked. Beside it was a small cabinet which held a key. The instructions above it said "BREAK GLASS FOR KEY".

"I need something to break the glass," Theo said quickly.

"Move." Angela ran over and hit the glass with the butt of the gun in her hand. The glass shattered instantly. Theo took out the key and opened the cabinet. Taking the nozzle in his left hand, he heaved off the rest of the hose with his right. It was heavy and he couldn't hold it, so he dropped it to the floor. Holding the nozzle, Theo and Angela ran to where Tom and Robbie were still fighting.

Both of their faces were covered with blood and one of Tom's eyes had swollen shut. Theo looked down at the nozzle. How did it work?

"It turns on from over there. I'll do it," Angela said.

She ran over to the fire cabinet and began to turn the large tap beneath the hose.

Theo gripped the hose tightly as he watched Angela turn the tap. Holding it away from him, he pointed it straight at the two struggling men on the ground. The hose coughed. It gurgled. It spluttered. A tiny trickle of water ran out over the end of the hose and dripped pathetically to the floor.

"Angela, nothing's happening," Theo called out.

"I'm turning it," Angela called back.

Tom lay groaning on the floor, his face a mass of bruises. Robbie started to stand up…

"Today, Angela! Today!" Theo urged.

"I'm doing my best," Angela snapped.

She was still facing the tap, turning it this way and that, trying to figure out what was wrong. Robbie was on his feet now, and was slowly advancing on Theo like a man-eating tiger ready to pounce.

"It's not working," Angela said un-necessarily.

Theo couldn't wait any longer. He yelled, "Angela, shift!" Theo threw the nozzle end of the hose at Robbie in sheer desperation.

Robbie sprang to one side. The hose missed him completely and hit the floor. But before he could take another step, the hose suddenly lurched up, turned back on itself with the force of the water funnelling down it and doused Robbie from the back of his head to his heels.

Robbie spun, his arms raised ready to sort out his new opponent. When he saw it was just a hose, he turned back to Theo, his expression thunderous. This was it. Theo thought Robbie was going to get him for sure. But just at that moment, two policemen emerged from the side doors, followed by Ricky. Robbie looked around desperately for somewhere to hide. Tom stuck out his foot and tripped up Robbie, sending him flying. One of the policemen ran to the main entrance and opened it up. Within moments, cars were screeching to a halt outside the museum, their sirens wailing, their lights flashing. Soon the main hall was swarming with police, most of them busy trying to subdue Robbie, who was fighting back like a cornered rat.

"Are you kids all right? Are you hurt? Do you need to go to hospital?" a policeman asked Angela and Theo, after turning off the fire hose, which was drenching the floor.

Theo shook his head, then handed over the bullets in his hand. Angela handed over the gun without saying a word.

"How did you get here so fast?" Theo asked.

"We've been on special alert ever since the Astral Collection arrived at the museum," the policeman explained. "Though I must admit, we thought the alarm going off was just a false alarm until your friend over there found us by the entrance and told us what was going on. If you're all sure you're all right, we'll need you down at the station for your statements."

"Let me go! LET ME GO!" Tom was struggling to get free from the policeman and policewoman who held him by his arms. "Angela, help me."

Theo turned. Tom pulled even harder to be free.

"You're making a mistake. Angela, t-tell them I don't have anything to do with these men. Tell them I came here with you. Tell them I was trying to stop the robbery."

"Is that true?" the policewoman who held Tom asked.

Angela stared up at her brother, without saying a word.

"Angela…?" Tom said desperately.

"Is that true, Angela?" the policewoman prompted.

The silence in the main hall was deafening as all eyes were turned on Angela.

"I… No," Angela whispered. "He was with Robbie and Dylan trying to steal the Astral Collection."

"Angela…" At Tom's shocked voice, Angela burst into tears.

Theo put his arm around Angela's shoulder. "Don't cry," he said, softly. "It's OK. It's over now."

"Angela…" Tom's voice held sad resignation.

"I'm sorry, Tom. I'm sorry. But I don't want to live like this any more – scared all the time," Angela sobbed.

They watched each other, before Tom was pulled away by his police escort.

"You'll find another member of the gang called Scott in the warehouse at 117 Buzan Road. He's in the basement," Theo told the policeman at his side.

"What's your name, son?" the policeman asked.

"Theo Mosley. And this is Angela. And this is my best friend, Ricky," Theo said as Ricky came running up.

"I'm Sergeant Goldstein," said the policeman. "Taking your statements should be interesting. I mean, how did you even get in here?"

"The same way they did. Angela's brother is a security guard here at the museum,"

Theo explained. "He's the one who let them in via the delivery entrance."

"The other guard on duty was tied up by Robbie. He's in one of the rooms over there," Ricky panted.

"Hang on. Haven't I seen you somewhere before?" The sergeant scrutinized Ricky.

"Ricky's been missing since Friday and..." Theo began to tell Sergeant Goldstein.

"I'm the one who's been missing. Let me tell it," Ricky demanded.

"Ricky Burridge..." Sergeant Goldstein whistled. "I thought I recognized you. We've been searching for you for days."

"You have?" Ricky asked.

"Let's get all of you down to the station," said Sergeant Goldstein. "And the first thing I'm going to do, Ricky, is call your mum."

20 Forgive me

23:48hrs Tuesday, 20th May

I don't have much time. There's a policewoman outside my door waiting to take me
out of here. I begged them to let me stay here
by myself. This is my home. But all the
grown-ups at the police station said I was too
young to be by myself. The policewoman outside says my social worker will process me
tomorrow. She makes it sound like I'm a roll
of film or a tin of peas or something, rather
than a person.

I'm writing this now 'cause I don't know
when I'll next get an opportunity to sit down
and write.

Tom's in a police cell.

So are the others. I don't care about them. Only Tom. He's in a police cell and I put him there. He wanted me to tell the police that he had nothing to do with Robbie and the others. How I wish I had now. How I wish... If I had to do it all over again, I'd say whatever Tom wanted me to say.

But it's too late.

Tom's in a police cell and I'm on my way to a home. Maybe one day I'll look back and think I did the right thing. I hope so. Then maybe this aching pain in my chest will go away.

I've got to go now. The policewoman's knocking on my door.

I'm sorry, Tom. I hope you'll forgive me. You're my brother and I love you but I'm so very tired. I just wanted it all to end. I just wanted it all behind us so we could go home and not jump every time there's a knock at the door or we pass a policeman. That's all. Please understand.

And ... and forgive me.

21 THREE WEEKS LATER

Theo sat with his head in his hands, staring at his essay. Only Mrs Daltry could take what was probably going to be the most exciting adventure of his life and turn it into boring, dull homework. The class had been told to write about the most exciting or frightening thing that had ever happened to them. Mrs Daltry was particularly keen for Theo to write about what she called "his adventures". She said he should write down every detail, every moment, but how could he? It hadn't been a fun adventure for Ricky and there were things that had happened between Angela and her brother Tom which weren't really his to tell. He'd tried writing down those bits but it just didn't feel right so he'd screwed up the first two drafts and now here he was with his third attempt and he didn't like this one any better. It made it seem as if he'd done everything himself. And he hadn't.

Downstairs the doorbell rang.

"Don't let that be another reporter," Theo murmured.

At first, reporters knocking on the door at all hours had seemed exciting. Truth to tell, it made Theo feel kind of important, but the novelty had worn off by the end of the first week. Now the reporters were just a pain in every bodily part!

Well, if it was a reporter, Mum and Dad would soon sort him or her out! They'd had enough of reporters too, especially those who wouldn't take no for an answer – which was ninety-nine per cent of them.

Theo leaned across his small table to push up his window. Maybe some fresh air would help him think straight because his essay was driving him nuts! And it had to be given in the following morning so time was running out. Theo had to make a decision about what to write and stick to it.

"Hi. Can I come in?" Ricky popped his head round the door.

" 'Course. You don't have to ask." Theo beckoned him in.

"What're you up to?" Ricky smiled, strolling over.

"I'm doing the essay Mrs Daltry told us to write," said Theo. "She didn't even let me decide for myself what I'd write about. She just told me to write about what happened at the Irving Museum."

Ricky's smile faded.

"You OK?" Theo asked.

Ricky shrugged. "Sure. Mrs Daltry said I could write about whatever I wanted. I don't have to write … to write about the same as you."

"So what did you write about?" asked Theo.

"I haven't done it yet." Ricky shrugged again.

"Are you going to?"

"I don't know." Ricky began to walk around the room aimlessly. He touched this, he shifted that until he came to stand by Theo's table again.

"Ricky, are you OK?" Theo asked, concerned.

"I guess. Yeah. Sure. I'm great. Why wouldn't I be? Mum lets me have anything I want now. I only have to ask – except she doesn't let me out of her sight and she wants to take me everywhere. She walked me over here and she told me to phone her when I'm ready to leave and she'll come and pick me up."

"She's just worried, that's all."

"Yeah, but she doesn't realize that every time she insists on taking me where I want to go, all she does is bring it all back. She won't let me forget what happened."

"Why don't you tell her that then?"

"I've tried. She won't listen."

"Then make her listen. Tell her until she hears you. Even my mum wanted to take me everywhere that first week after it happened, and I wasn't the one who was ... who was kidnapped."

"No, you weren't," Ricky said faintly. "Did I tell you? One of those tabloids that Mum always called 'tacky' offered her a lot of money for my story."

"Are you going to do it?"

"I think ... no." Ricky's voice grew more and more quiet. "I still have nightmares, you know. I dream that I've lost my hands and my feet and my mouth and I can't speak or shout or anything. Two nights ago I had a dream that there was nothing left of me but my brain and my two eyes staring out, and try as I could, I couldn't make anyone understand what I was thinking."

"I ... I'm sorry." Theo mentally cursed himself for being so ineffectual, but he really didn't know what else to say.

This was the first time Ricky had said a word to Theo about what had happened to him. Theo knew he needed to talk. Hell! He'd spent the last three weeks thinking about very little else himself, but recently he'd begun to wonder if maybe he'd dreamt bits of it. The bad bits. And then he'd see Ricky's face and the shadows in his eyes and know he hadn't.

"I'm sorry, Ricky," Theo repeated.

"Yeah, well so am I." Ricky started wandering around the room again.

"Maybe the dreams will stop," Theo suggested.

"And maybe they won't," Ricky said with sudden bitterness. "Those five days when I was a prisoner were the worst days I'll ever have in my life. I'm not going to put them in a stupid story for Mrs Daltry or relive them so some lousy tabloid can sell a few more papers. I just want to forget it. I just want… I just want…" Ricky's face contorted as he tried to blink back the tears threatening to embarrass him. But it didn't work.

"Sorry," Ricky sniffed, wiping his hand over his eyes. But the tears didn't stop.

Theo stood up, watching his friend unhappily.

"T-They kept me tied up all the time. They

only released my hands and feet to let me go to the loo. They only released my hands and took the tape off my mouth so I could eat. I even had to sleep tied up." Ricky started to shake as he remembered. "Robbie… Robbie threatened to shoot me if I tried to run away. He dared me to try – he said he needed the target practice."

Theo gritted his teeth, fury blazing like an inferno through his body.

"I'm sorry I'm crying. I'll stop in a minute," Ricky sniffed.

Theo wished he could think of something to say, but instead he just stood by his table feeling totally useless. He made his way over to his friend and sat down next to him.

"You cry if you want to, Ricky," Theo said. "There'd be something very wrong with you if you didn't cry after everything you've been through."

Ricky buried his face in his hands and wept. After a moment's indecision, Theo put his arm around Ricky's shoulder and hugged him.

22 FRIENDS

It was incredible but true. Mrs Daltry was even more boring than usual! Somehow she managed to make the subject of how the Earth was formed as interesting as watching fingernails grow! Ricky nudged Theo in the ribs. Theo nudged him back. They both glanced at each other and wrinkled up their noses. The classroom door opened.

Theo gasped when he saw who came in. A gasp echoed by Ricky – and everyone else in the class.

It was Angela.

"Hello, Angela. Take your seat," said Mrs Daltry.

Her head bowed, Angela made her way over to her old table and sat down. Theo and Ricky looked at each other, stunned. What was Angela doing back here? She hadn't been seen since the Irving Museum business. Theo looked across the classroom at her. She looked gaunt and miserable. Theo had seen that look before – on Ricky's face.

After that, everything Mrs Daltry said about how the Earth was formed didn't even get as far as going in one ear and out the other. It just bounced straight off Theo's and Ricky's heads. Neither of them could concentrate. Angela had all their attention.

Years passed – at least that's what it felt like! – before the buzzer finally sounded. Mrs Daltry was first out of the class, a liquorice allsort already on its way to her mouth. Others in the class began to amble out. Angela was busy packing her bag. Theo noticed how she never looked up, never caught anyone's eye, even when they spoke to her. She'd answer in monosyllables, still packing her bag.

"Come on." Theo nudged Ricky and they both went over to Angela.

"Hello, Angela," Theo said quietly.

Angela glanced up quickly. Her glance down again was even faster.

"Hello, Theo." There was a pause. "Ricky."

Theo looked at Ricky. His face was expressionless.

"So how're you doing?" Theo asked.

"Fine," Angela replied, her nose buried in her bag.

"Are you going to be in our class permanently?" said Theo.

"Yes," said Angela.

Theo sighed inwardly. She wasn't making this very easy.

"What happened to your brother?" Ricky asked.

Angela looked up, her eyes glistening, her expression hostile. "He's been remanded in custody. They all have. So go ahead and gloat."

"I'm not gloating," Ricky said quietly. "Do you live by yourself now then?"

"No. I'm living with my new foster parents."

"What're they like?" Theo asked.

"What d'you care?" Angela said belligerently.

"Just asking," Theo replied.

"Listen. I know you two hate me and well, I don't care. I hate you too. And I know you've told the whole class about me and my brother and they all hate me as well. Well, it wasn't my fault. I tried to stop Tom – I *did*. And I'm not going to apologize any more. I'm not."

Theo opened his mouth to speak but Ricky got in first.

"Now, you listen. We don't hate you. And we haven't told anyone in the class a thing, have we, Theo? All they know is what they read in the papers and saw on telly," Ricky said. "And no one's asking you to apologize for anything. It wasn't your fault. In fact if it wasn't for you, Theo couldn't have rescued me."

"But I was the one who wrote out the dare which got you captured in the first place." Angela stood up, letting her bag drop to the floor. "You hate me for that at least."

"At first I did," Ricky admitted. "But you wouldn't have written it if you'd known how things were going to turn out. I know that now."

"Why're you being so nice to me?" Angela asked suspiciously.

"Because I know what it's like to be alone and scared," Ricky said simply. "And I can see from your face that that's how you feel."

"I don't want you to feel sorry for me," Angela fumed.

"I don't. I think you're feeling sorry enough for yourself. You don't need any help from me," said Ricky.

"Well, I don't need you or anyone else for that matter. I'm doing just fine on my own."

Ricky sighed. "Suit yourself. I just thought we could be friends, that's all. Come on, Theo. Let's go for lunch."

Ricky walked off without another word. Theo looked from Ricky to Angela helplessly. With a shrug, he turned and ran to catch up with Ricky.

"Ricky…?" Angela stopped them just as they reached the door. "Can I … can I go to lunch with you two?"

Ricky smiled. "Sure. If you like."

Angela picked up her bag and ran to catch up with them.

"This doesn't mean I like you two or anything," Angela said.

" 'Course not. It doesn't mean we like you either," Ricky agreed.

"But we've all got to eat," Theo added.

Theo was the first to smile, with Ricky, then Angela joining in reluctantly.

"Come on. I'm starving," said Ricky.

And they left the classroom together, discussing just how boring Mrs Daltry had been that morning.

23 NOWHERE TO GO BUT UP

19:00hrs Monday, 16th June

Today wasn't as bad as I thought it was going to be. I had a long chat with Ricky and Theo at lunch time and we all walked home together. Colin and some others came over to me when I was eating my lunch and tried to ask me all sorts of questions but Theo and Ricky weren't having any. I didn't have to say a word. Theo called Colin a nosy doof and two-thirds and told him to bog off or else – and from the look on Theo's face, everyone could see he wasn't joking.

It's funny but when I first joined Mrs

Daltry's class, I thought Ricky was big and brash and didn't have much going for him and I must admit, I thought Theo was a bit of a wimp. It just goes to show, doesn't it. I got them both completely wrong.

I still miss Tom desperately. Marian, my new foster mum, says she'll take me to see him if I want. Tom wrote to me, asking me to visit him but I don't know. I'm not sure. To be honest, I'm scared. I don't know how he thinks of me. In his letter he said I'm still his favourite sister and he hopes he's still my favourite brother. I miss him so much. I want everything to go back to the way it was and yet I'm glad it's not like that any more. That makes it sound like I don't even know my own mind and to be honest, I'm not sure I do. Everything is still a jumble in my head.

D'you know, I look back and I still can't believe that all this started with a dare. Ricky was right about that. If I'd known what would come of it I would never, ever have written it. I would've broken my fingers first.

Tom's in prison and I'm all alone and I feel

like I've no one to talk to and nowhere to go. At least I felt like that till today. Marian and George — he's my foster dad — practically frog-marched me to school. What with not feeling well and having to get myself sorted out, I haven't been to school in four weeks. I didn't want to go back today — certainly not to the same school where everyone knows about me, but like I said, it wasn't as bad as I thought it would be.

For the first time in a long, long time I think I may have made two real friends. I guess I should look forward now, not back. What's done is done. What I said before, about having nowhere to go, it's not true. I've just realized. The only place I can go from here is up.

Hippo Fantasy

Lose yourself in a whole new world, a world where anything is possible – from wizards and dragons, to time travel and new civilizations . . . Gripping, thrilling, scary and funny by turns, these Hippo Fantasy titles will hold you captivated to the very last page.

The Night of Wishes
Michael Ende (author of *The Neverending Story*)

Malcolm and the Cloud-Stealer
Douglas Hill

The Wednesday Wizard
Sherryl Jordan

Ratspell
Paddy Mounter

Rowan of Rin
Emily Rodda

The Practical Princess
Jay Williams

The Outfit

Robert Swindells

**"Faithful, fearless, full of fun,
Winter, summer, rain or sun,
One for five, and five for one –
THE OUTFIT!"**

*Meet The Outfit – Jillo, Titch, Mickey and Shaz. Share in
their adventures as they fearlessly investigate any mystery,
and injustice, that comes their way . . .*

Move over, Famous Five, The Outfit are here!

The Secret of Weeping Wood

The Outfit are determined to discover the truth about the
eerie crying, coming from scary Weeping Wood. Is the
wood really haunted?

We Didn't Mean To, Honest!

The marriage of creepy Kenneth Kilchaffinch to snooty
Prunella could mean that Froglet Pond, and all its
wildlife, will be destroyed. So it's up to The Outfit to
make sure the marriage is off . . . But how?

Kidnap at Denton Farm

Farmer Denton's new wind turbine causes a protest
meeting in Lenton, and The Outfit find themselves in
the thick of it. But a *kidnap* is something they didn't
bargain for . . .

The Ghosts of Givenham Keep

What is going on at spooky Givenham Keep? It can't be
haunted, can it? The Outfit are just about to find out . . .